Praise for Meg Maguire's
Trespass

"*Trespass* is beautifully written, a powerful drama that will stay with you. I won't reveal the ending, but be ready to shed some happy tears."

~ *Long and Short Reviews*

"I just didn't want to put the book down..."

~ *Fiction Vixen Book Reviews*

"This is the second hero and book by this author that I've loved this year. After this one, she's going to my autobuy list."

~ *Book Utopia*

"Maguire tells of two needy people who rely on each other for vastly different reasons. The tension mounts as Sarah's story is revealed and the couple begins to understand their feelings."

~ *RT Book Reviews*

Look for these titles by *Meg Maguire*

Now Available:

The Reluctant Nude
Trespass
Headstrong

Trespass

Meg Maguire

SAMHAIN PUBLISHING

Samhain Publishing, Ltd.
11821 Mason Montgomery Road, 4B
Cincinnati, OH 45249
www.samhainpublishing.com

First Samhain Publishing, Ltd. electronic publication: July 2011
First Samhain Publishing, Ltd. print publication: June 2012

Dedication

I'd like to thank Kat and Rebecca Duncan, and Kathy and everyone else at Ironstone Farm for letting me muck around and pester them with my endless questions about horses and firearms. Thanks also to Liz, for her city-girl perspective on Montana (and its men). And thanks as always to my husband, a pied among blue-bars.

Chapter One

By the bluish glow of a nearly full moon, Sarah spotted her first sign of civilization in an hour—an unlit house on this endless, lonely stretch of dirt road in Nowheresville, Montana. She picked up her pace, arm wrapped around her middle to cradle her wounded side. She kept her eyes locked on the shapes ahead, the trapezoid of a roof, the ladderlike stripes of a porch railing.

Her progress along the gravel rang out in the still night, uneven footsteps like seconds ticking by on a broken clock. The darkness and quiet didn't scare her. If anything, their purity was a comfort now, a merciful change from the noise and the buzzing, yellow bulbs of the bus stations Sarah had been sleeping in for the past three weeks, the sickly light seeping beneath the doors in every rundown women's shelter between here and Buffalo. Between this dead-silent road and the night her entire life had collapsed. The night she'd become a fugitive.

One minute she'd been camped out on a barstool with a friend, watching baseball, nursing her second beer. Then, a phone call. A short run to an old friend's house, moments later the snap decision that ended her world as she knew it, sent her out into the unknown without so much as a change of clothes. She'd covered nearly two thousand miles, on bus and foot mainly. It'd only taken a couple of stints as a hitchhiker for Sarah to conclude it wasn't the way for a single woman to travel. Granted, the knife she'd had held to her throat by the second—and last—driver she'd ever flagged down would only leave a tiny scar on the outside, probably some deeper damage to her psyche. The buckshot presently lodged in her side from a run-in with a territorial farm owner... Now that injury seemed poised to linger. Whoever had given her the impression that people from postcard-pretty places like Montana would be kind and welcoming... Well, next time she'd ask for proof.

She drew close to the house, a small one-story with a long wooden structure attached to its far side. She'd slept on a bench in the Billings bus depot the previous night and doubted crashing in some stranger's barn could be much worse. Cows and horses were unlikely to try to rob or sexually harass her—

Barks shattered the silence. Sarah stopped dead in the road, yards from the lonely house. Out of darkness shot two bodies, pointed ears alert, teeth glinting in the moonlight.

Russ woke to the sound of canine alarm, his dogs barking their ever-loving heads off in the front yard. He squinted at his dresser and the glowing numbers on his clock. Nine past one.

"Not a skunk," he prayed. "Not a skunk, not a skunk—"

A woman's shriek joined the chorus.

Blood chilled in an instant, Russ launched himself out of bed and scrambled through the dark house, grabbing his rifle along the way. He hit the switch for the porch light and burst out the front door and down the steps.

The two German Shepherds looked wild in the low, dingy light, dutifully guarding an inexplicable woman standing in front of Russ's house. She seemed paralyzed, frozen between the glaring dogs and their two sets of intimidating teeth, arms held up as if someone had a gun trained on her. Which come to think of it, Russ basically did.

"It's okay." He said it mainly to the dogs and their bodies relaxed. "Kit. Tulah." The dogs looked at him. "Fuck off." He gave Tulah a whap on the butt and waved his hand, and she trotted obediently around the back of the house. Kit offered the woman's waist a final breathy snort then reluctantly followed.

Russ turned to the woman, still paralyzed in profile. "Sorry about that. They won't bother you."

She turned, eyes wide. She lowered her arms and wrapped them around her middle. She was skinny, no older than thirty Russ guessed, with light brown hair draped over narrow shoulders. She had on jeans and sneakers and a long-sleeved shirt...no bag, no coat, no flashlight, no explanation for turning up at the edge of Russ's far-flung property at one a.m.

He was about to demand one when he suddenly registered his own getup, boxers and a rifle.

"Hey," he said.

No reply.

"Um... Hang on a minute." Russ left her to trot up the steps. He ditched the .22, jogged to his room and tugged on jeans and a T-shirt. She was right where he'd left her when he went back outside, her eyes aimed in the direction the dogs had disappeared.

"Hey," he said again, clomping down the steps. "You okay?"

She nodded, way too quick.

"You break down someplace?" Russ looked at her shirt, her locked arms not hiding the dark stain along one side of her waist. "Oh my God." He came close. He touched her forearms, tugging gently.

She locked them tighter. "Don't."

He eased into his firm, soothing work voice. "I'm a doctor. Are you bleeding?"

"No. Not anymore."

9

She and Russ exchanged awkward eye contact as he attempted to pry her stubborn arms apart.

"I'm not gonna hurt you," he said. "And I don't care what you're doing here in the middle of the night, okay? Just let me see where you're bleeding."

She swallowed, jaw twitching as she considered it.

"Please. I won't hurt you, I swear."

She let her arms drop, revealing a mottled bloodstain at her waist.

"Good God. Come inside," Russ said, not an invitation. He steered her firmly by the shoulder, up the steps and inside, shutting the door on the chilly September air.

The woman stood at the edge of the open den, looking around Russ's modest ranch house.

He tucked his hands in his pockets in an attempt to look nonthreatening. "Can I ask what happened to you?"

She glanced around a few seconds longer then met his gaze squarely, the rigid stubbornness seeming to abandon her posture. "I got shot."

"Shot?" Russ felt his eyebrows trying to jump clean off his face. He stepped to her, no permission requested. "Lift it up. Let me see."

She eased the cream-colored shirt up and over her head. Underneath she had on a purple tank top, the kind with skinny straps and a narrow lacy border—the sort of garment women probably had a special name for, one Russ had surely never heard of. She peeled that off too, stripped to her putty-colored bra. Russ hadn't seen a near-naked woman in about seven years, not in person anyhow. He'd always hoped he might find himself roughly in this position, but the reality of this moment wasn't anywhere near as thrilling as his expectations. He looked at her and saw pale skin riddled from the waist to the ribs with red pits and scrapes, saw nothing but a patient. Still, buckshot might not take so kindly to a friendly smack. He went to his closet and gathered some wool blankets from the shelf, grabbed one of the pillows off his bed. Nicole stood nearby as he got the couch set up.

"Could I get a glass of water?"

"Of course." He went to the cupboards and filled her a mug from the tap.

"Thanks." She accepted the cup, downing it in two gulps.

"Like I said, help yourself. And the bathroom's there," he added, pointing. "If you want warm water you better beat me to it in the morning."

A genuine smile overtook her face, eyes crinkling, two dimples punctuating either corner of her wide lips. Russ watched her refill her cup before settling into the pile of blankets with slow, cautious movements, testing her injuries.

"You sleep tight now," Russ said. "Come knock if you need anything."

"I will, thanks."

He nodded, not quite willing to meet her eyes, the strangeness of their new acquaintance sinking in now that his adrenaline had faded. He offered the wall to the left of her face an anxious smile, clicked off the lamp and closed himself in his bedroom.

Chapter Two

A bomb exploding couldn't have woken Sarah before noon. It was the sunlight that eventually did the job, coaxing her eyes open and ushering in strange surroundings, and a sensation of comfort so foreign she sat bolt upright with fear. She squeaked out a cry from the pain that shot up her side.

She held her ribs, glancing around the sun-drenched den of Russ's small house. It was Russ, right? Yes. Russell Gray, farmer-doctor-man, the guy who'd come at her in his underwear holding a rifle, called off the dogs, picked buckshot pellets out of her and given her a feast's worth of cereal and a shirt to sleep in. And she was...? Nicole now. Not Sarah, Nicole. You'd think after more than a week of living that lie she'd be better at remembering.

The clock on the wall above her said it was twelve thirty. She tossed the covers aside, chilly autumn air tensing her body.

She made it to her achy feet, found the bathroom and a clean, threadbare towel folded in half-assed male fashion in the cupboard. Russ Gray didn't have much in the way of toiletries, but shampoo and soap and toothpaste were all she really wanted. The shower started up with a couple of loud thumps, the water coming strong and hot and sputtery. She stripped and climbed into the rounded, cramped enamel tub, just about dying of pleasure as the spray hit her. She remembered her bandage and gently peeled it from her waist, setting it on the will. Uh-huh. My best to Andrea. Bye." He pushed another button and set the phone on the table.

"Horse?" she asked.

"Alpaca, actually."

"Oh. Neat." Sarah wasn't actually sure what an alpaca looked like. Like a goat in a fur coat, she guessed. "Well, if my cuts are looking good I guess I should probably get out of your hair."

Russ's eyebrows shot up. "Oh?"

"You've been really kind," she said, gaze jumping to his open case.

"Can I talk you out of leaving so soon?" He locked his arms over his chest, the gesture giving him a bit of extra authority, as though he'd hung an invisible stethoscope around his neck. "I think you're going to be fine, but I'll be honest with you... I don't know what you're up to that you've managed to get shot and held at knife-point, and I'm not all that eager to send you back out into it. I wish you'd think about staying a few days."

"I don't have much money and I wouldn't want to be a mooch." Her body tensed, and she waited to see if he was about to step close and offer to let her pay him in *other ways*.

Instead he smiled his kind smile again. "You wouldn't be a mooch. I have plenty of food, and you can repay me with the company. Maybe I'll get a couple drinks in you, and you'll tell me all about what brought you here." He grinned hopefully.

"Don't hold your breath. But yeah...I guess I'd like that." A couple days in a warm house with real food, a couch to sleep on and hot showers whenever she wanted, no charge? It sucked, lying to this nice man, but for safety and comfort, she could stay Nicole a little longer. "I'll stick around, if that's really okay with you. On one condition."

"Okay."

"You let me do something to help. Dishes or laundry or dusting. Anything."

Russ laughed. "You hinting something about my homemaking skills?"

"No, not at all. Just, you know, stuff I know how to do. I won't be much use in a barn or stable or whatever, even if I wasn't hurt."

He nodded. "Sure. I'll put you to work."

She stepped forward and offered her hand, liking the feel of Russ's firm shake. "Cool. Deal." She glanced around his home again, trying to remember what day of the week it even was. Then again, Russ likely did the same things every day. Animals probably didn't take weekends off from being needy.

"How does your schedule work, anyway?" she asked.

"Get up, take care of the horses, feed the dogs, fix this or that until somebody calls. Go out on a job or two. Mail out invoices, muck around on the phone with insurance companies. Thrilling stuff."

"Same thing every day?"

He shrugged. "Sort of. Then again, every day's different."

"Like when some random woman turns up while you're trying to sleep?"

"Yeah, that can happen. Keeps things interesting."

"Is this a busy time for you? September?" God, September already.

"Fall's pretty easy. Spring is insanity between lambing and calving. I need the rest of the year to catch my breath." He looked around the room. "Did you eat yet?"

She shook her head.

"Can I cook you something? Eggs or pancakes or...?"

She laughed. "Nobody's made me pancakes in years."

"It's just the powdered stuff."

"God, like I'm in a position to be picky. Go ahead. Pancakes sound amazing."

She watched as this dusty stranger cooked a skillet of bacon, mixed batter, heaped her a plate of pancakes and rashers, and set a metal can of syrup before her on the table.

"Wow, thanks."

He assembled his own plate and took a seat across from her. They ate in silence, her wolfing her food down once again, knowing she must look like some feral child rescued from the woods but unable to resist the impulse when faced with another free feast. She finished before Russ was halfway through his own food.

She got up and brought them each a fresh cup of coffee. "Milk or sugar?"

"Black's fine, thanks."

She splashed milk into her own mug and took her seat. She noticed Russ's eyes. They were a weird color, pale grayish-green, his pupil a tiny black dot from the sun streaming through the window beside them. She looked at his faint crow's feet, the fine lines drawn across his brow. Just a few grays hiding in the overgrown brown hair tucked behind his ears. *Thirty-four,* she guessed. "Can I ask how old you are?"

Russ took a sip then set his cup down. "Thirty-six."

"Ah-ha."

"You?"

She had to think about it for a second, conjuring Nicole's borrowed birthday from her memory. "Thirty-two." Younger in actuality, though she felt about a hundred.

He made a face. "Wow, I wouldn't have guessed—"

"No kids or anything?" she cut in.

"No kids."

"Me neither. And no farmer's wife?"

He smiled tightly. "I wouldn't dare call myself a farmer. And no, no wife. Not anymore, anyhow."

"Oh. How long were you married?"

He sponged at his syrup with a forkful of pancake. "Just over three years."

"Ah. Was country life not everything she thought it would be?"

Russ chewed and swallowed, strange pale irises aimed over the fields past the window. "I'm not divorced. My wife died."

A block of ice dropped into her belly. "Oh God, I'm sorry. That was so rude of me to assume you're divorced."

He met her eyes. "It's okay. And it's been seven years. I'm not delicate about it."

She toyed with her fork. "Can I ask what happened to her?"

He nodded, gaze drifting back to his plate. "She got thrown from a horse. Broke her neck."

Sarah put her fingertips to her syrupy lips.

Russ laughed, presumably at her fraught expression. "I'm okay about it. Really. She's been gone for longer than we were together, now."

"That's so...sad."

He frowned thoughtfully, as though contemplating whether or not to get all philosophical about his dead wife.

"Were you there, when it happened?" she asked.

"No. Horse came back alone."

"And you're the one who...found her?"

Russ nodded.

"Was it one of the two horses—"

"No." He shook his head. "I'm not one to blame an animal for doing what's in its nature, but that's too far even for me. I sold that horse." He stood and took their plates to the sink.

She nodded, somber and unseen, feeling sad for this man, way too young to be seven years widowed. Way too kind.

Russ moved to the window, pushing the sill up to shout at where one of the dogs had its feet up on the wooden fence, barking at the horses. "Kitten!"

The dog looked to him, busted, dropped to the ground and trotted away. Russ closed the window and rolled his eyes.

"Kitten?" she asked, smirking at him.

"My wife named her. Because of..." He drew invisible triangle ears above his own head. "When she was a puppy. That, and she used to eat yarn."

"Gotcha. She wasn't much of a kitten last night."

"They wouldn't have hurt you, you know. They're just territorial."

"Like their owner?" she asked, and gave the handle of his rifle, leaning against the bottom of the window frame, the gentlest of kicks.

"Careful."

"Sorry."

"Well, I'm sorry too," he said, "about them scaring you. And you probably weren't in the mood to have some crazy man in his underwear come running toward you with a loaded weapon."

She laughed at the visual, though at the time it hadn't been funny at all. At the time all she'd registered were two sets of teeth vibrating with angry growls and a strange man advancing on her, his near-naked body stark and threatening in the yellow porch lights.

"Weirder things have happened to me in the last couple weeks," she concluded with a shrug.

"I won't ask."

"Thanks."

They shared a brief but awkward silence before Russ went to the sink to start the dishes. Sarah walked over and pushed at his arm until he stepped aside. "Let me do that."

She felt Russ's eyes on her and the scrutiny didn't bother her. Frankly she wished she had a bit more to offer him than a tangle of wet hair and her battered, underfed body draped in his ill-fitting shirt. That the idea of a strange man sizing her up wasn't a source of panic was wondrous in itself.

She washed and rinsed the dishes, handing them to Russ to dry and put them in their places. She liked the soft-looking brown hair on his forearms, the flex of his tendons and the strong shapes of his fingers, his weird mix of rugged and clean, cowboy and doctor.

"So your horses," she said. "Do you actually ride them or are they patients or...?"

"They're mine. I ride them most days, though not as much as I'd like." He took a cup from her and wiped it dry.

"They aren't like, work horses, right? They don't pull equipment or anything?"

He laughed. "Where in the heck are you from? Manhattan?"

"Not Montana, that's for sure."

"Well the days of plough horses are over around here. They're just for riding, those two."

"What are they called?" she asked.

"Lizzie and Mitch."

"Are they...boyfriend and girlfriend? Like lovers or whatever?"

Russ set down the fork he'd just dried, gripping the counter's edge and sinking into a silent, body-quaking laugh. He straightened up, wiping his eyes. "Lovers," he wheezed.

She smiled, embracing her own ignorance. No point having an ego with the man who'd picked buckshot out of her. "You know what I mean."

"No, Mitch is a gelding."

"What's a gelding?"

Russ made a snipping motion with his fingers at groin-level.

"Oh, ouch."

He nodded and accepted the plate she handed him.

"That sucks for him," she said. "Do *you* ever have to do that? You know." She made the finger-scissor motion.

"Sure."

"You ever worry the ghosts of a thousand jilted, nutless horses will come back to haunt you?" She pointed her eyes at his belt.

Russ made a nervous face. "Not sure I like the way you think, Nicole."

She swallowed, not entirely comfortable hearing him address her with such familiarity, and not by that name, certainly. The warm rapport faltered, then she banished the unwelcome anxiety. She suspected she was safe here...and if she wasn't, it didn't help to think about it.

She handed him the last dish and shut off the faucet. "Did you grow up around here?"

He shook his head. "I grew up in Idaho, but my great-grandfather and my grandfather lived pretty close, about forty miles from here." He nodded toward the back of the house as though this might mean somewhere to her.

"Were they farmers?"

"They were both farriers—you know, they shoed horses. They did pretty much everything I do, just without the formality of a license."

"So all this is like, in your blood?"

"I guess. Must skip random generations, since my dad's a dentist." Russ drained the coffee pot into their mugs and switched the machine off. He wandered over to take a seat on his ugly old burnt-sienna easy chair and Sarah followed, lowering herself carefully onto the couch, a palm on her tender ribs.

"Can I ask what *you* do?" he asked. "When you're not hitchhiking and eating me out of house and home?"

Her good mood cooled again. "I'd rather not say."

Russ held her eyes a moment, smiled in a sad, sympathetic way that she hated and loved equally.

She glanced around the room for a change of subject. "No TV?"

"Nope. No cable out here, plus I don't really care for it."

"Internet?"

Russ shook his head. "That one's a bit troublesome. I'd probably save myself a lot of time if I had it, but it's one of those things I just never get around to. If I really need it, I'll go to a neighbor's or head in to town and use the library's computers."

"Gotcha." Actually, no internet was a relief—a good excuse to stay in the dark about what might be happening back home, ignorant bliss about any efforts being made to find her. TV, though...she'd miss that, especially since she wouldn't be making the news, not way out in Montana. Oh well. There were other ways to stay distracted.

She drained her cup and set it on a side table, slapped her palms to her knees with finality. "So. Put me to work."

"Okay." He looked around the room, thinking. "How about laundry? You're probably missing your own clothes."

She nodded, a lie. If she never again saw those clothes she'd been living in these last three weeks, it'd be too soon. At least she'd been wearing sneakers and not heels when she'd wound up a fugitive. "Do you have a machine, or do I like go down to the river and scrub them against the rocks?"

He shot her an adorable, annoyed look. "There's a machine, smart-ass. You want to put those jeans in too?"

She looked down at the denim, stiff with dirt and sweat and whatever else lurked in the places she'd been sleeping. "Yeah."

Russ disappeared into his bedroom and emerged to toss her a pair of boxers. He headed to a drawer by the sink, coming back with a couple of safety pins.

"Thanks." She changed in the bathroom, hiding her wallet behind some junk in the cabinet beneath the sink. She felt eerily naked, braless under Russ's soft old work shirt, commando in his boxers, a breeze finding her through the threadbare cotton. The sensation was about twenty percent sexy, eighty percent dopey. She cinched the waist with a pin and closed the fly with the other. She walked back out into the den in her mismatched, borrowed plaids with her jeans tucked under one arm, bra and panties folded inside.

Russ carried his hamper out of his bedroom. Sarah followed him past the closed door to what she now assumed must be a time-capsule room full of wifely objects, stuff too painful to look at but even more painful to part with. Or who knew—maybe it was where he hid all his kinky bondage props. Kindness and practicality aside, Russ Gray could be anybody, with who-knew-what to hide.

He led her out the back door and down some steps to a garage-ish room that connected the house and the stable, full of shelves and tools and that fertile, horse-crappy farm smell. An ancient washer and dryer were parked in one corner. Russ set the hamper down and got the machine filling.

"I can handle the rest," she said, shooing him away. "Let me earn my keep." *Let me make this up to you,* she added, preemptive guilt twisting her gut. She knew when she moved on from here, she'd be indebted to Russ for more than just his

31

hospitality... Probably whatever cash he had in his wallet and some food for the road, things she prayed she'd be able to pay back one day, when and if her life ever settled down again.

Russ grabbed a box of detergent from a shelf and plunked it on the dryer. He left her alone, heading back inside.

She dumped some powder in the machine, and dropped in her jeans and underwear. She winced as she leaned in to grab things from the hamper—her own dirty, bloody camisole and shirt, Russ's jeans and underwear, socks and handkerchiefs, a seemingly endless supply of heather-gray T-shirts. She dropped the lid and trotted back up the steps into the house, past that door to the mystery room.

Russ was on the phone again, leaning over the kitchen table and jotting on a spiral pad. "Uh-huh... Just calfhood? How many, do you think? Sixty? Nope, no problem. I'll come first thing, a week from Tuesday... You too. Bye now." He set the phone down and made a few more notes.

"More balls to snip?" she asked.

Russ jumped and put a hand to his heart.

"Sorry," she said.

"Oh, don't be. I'm just not used to having company yet. Not the kind that talks. And no, no ball-snipping, smarty-pants. Boring old routine vaccinations."

She nodded. "So, what else can I do around here?"

He rubbed his chin as he considered it. "You ever brushed a horse?"

"No, never."

"Want to learn?" he asked, already heading for the back door again.

"Sure. They won't kick me, will they?"

Russ pulled his shoes on. "Not unless you do something to deserve it."

She swallowed.

He led her through to the tidy, stinky stable then trotted into the fenced-in area, coming back with the white and gray horse and tethering it to a post.

"This is Mitch," he said, running a hand over the huge animal's back.

"Hi, Mitch."

"Here." Russ grabbed a plastic tumbler full of carrots from a high shelf and she took one.

"Go on."

She held it to the horse's lips, met by a set of massive, dull teeth.

"Like this," Russ said as half the carrot disappeared. He opened her hand and lay what was left on her palm. "Keep it flat. Like that."

Mitch finished it off, and she stroked his nose with her other hand, the one thing she did know how to do with a horse.

"He likes you."

"Only 'cause I fed him," she said, petting his neck.

"Is that the only reason you like me?" Russ asked, and that tight little grin was flirtation if she'd ever seen it.

"Who said I like you?" she cut back, haughty.

"Oooh." He made a pained, low-blow face.

She laughed, keeping her eyes on Mitch's neck as she petted him. "I'll need to see what you make for dinner, first."

"Forget grooming—you're clearly gunning for castration duty."

She turned and smiled at him, a full-on fond, friendly grin she'd let him take for whatever he wanted.

Russ got her set up with a funny oval-shaped brush with rubber nubs instead of bristles, a currycomb. Sarah added it to her mental list of new rural vocab words. He showed her how to rub it in firm circles over Mitch's coat. He told her not to bend or crouch if it hurt too much, though she'd already decided to do the best damn horse-grooming job he'd ever seen and was willing to work for it.

While she brushed Mitch, Russ went to Lizzie and snapped reins onto what Sarah suspected was called a bridle.

"Are you going to ride?" she asked.

"Yup. Just a bit of exercise. Don't worry, I'm only going around the pen. I won't leave you alone to get stomped on." He led the horse into the dusty yard.

"Don't you need a saddle?"

"Nah, not for this."

"How do you get up there?" She dropped her arms and gave Russ her full attention, watching him check one of the horse's feet.

"You just jump."

The horse's back looked freaky-high. It seemed that even if Russ *could* toss himself up there, having a hundred and eighty-odd pounds of man suddenly land on you would surely piss a horse off.

"Jump? Up *there?*"

"Sure."

Sarah had a thought. She set the currycomb aside and grabbed Russ's hat from its hook on the wall, walking into the pen to hand it him. "Okay then, cowboy. Let's see it."

Russ grinned and propped the hat on his head, that squint and dimple just a cigarette shy of an ad campaign. He gave Lizzie a few pats, and with a hand on the ridge of her lower neck, he took two quick steps and swung himself on, smooth as another man might sink into a sports car.

"Wow," she said.

Russ arranged the reins and gave Lizzie a couple more gentle slaps. "Not really wow-worthy."

"If you say so."

She watched him lead the horse around in dusty circles, walking, then a bit faster.

Grooming Mitch took forever, mainly because Russ on horseback was so insanely distracting. It wasn't as romantic a scene as she might have imagined, not like the cover of a book or a slow-motion scene from a movie. Russ simply looked like a man doing a chore he very much enjoyed, the horse a strange amalgamation of riding mower and dog. His relationship with the animal seemed easy and familiar, its magic wrapped up in the mundane, not the mystical.

Sarah finished combing Mitch right around the time Russ hopped back down to the ground. He unclipped Lizzie's reins and left the horse to her own motives.

"How we doing?" he asked, hanging the reins on a nail.

"Done, I think."

He stepped close, lifting his hat off and setting it on Sarah's head. He blinked in the high western sun, gray-green eyes like aquarium glass. She swallowed, looking up at his face. He wasn't exceptionally tall, maybe five ten, but he seemed big and sturdy and solid just now, substantial and *real*. She wondered what his mouth tasted like. She took his hat off and turned it around in her hands, studying the mesh of the tight-woven straw.

Russ checked her work and she stole a whiff of his smell. It was tough to pick Russ's scent out from the fragrances of the stable, but she decided she could. She decided he smelled fantastic, like an old leather belt and the cork from a whiskey bottle.

"Very nice," he said, giving Mitch a final pat.

"Do I get a carrot?"

He smiled. "Actually, yeah. In a roundabout sort of way." He consulted the screen of his phone. "Well I don't know about you, Nicole..."

Unseen, she winced at the name.

"But I'm bushed. How about we call it a day?" He wiped his hands pointlessly on his filthy jeans.

"Yeah. Sounds good."

"It's only two o'clock but dinner's going to take a while, and what're Saturdays for if not laziness?"

Saturday. Good to know.

Russ brought Lizzie into the stable and they double-teamed her with the currycombs, then stocked both horses with fresh hay. Russ took his hat back and hung it in its place. Wandering around for a minute, he seemed to go through a mental checklist before they headed inside, with a brief pit stop to move the clothes to the dryer. They kicked their shoes off at the bottom of the steps, and Russ held the door open for her.

"You cook much?" he asked.

"Barely."

He closed the door behind them, shutting out that barn smell she'd nearly ceased to notice.

"You can cut potatoes though, right, city girl?"

She laughed. "Yeah. I can cut potatoes, cowboy."

"Great." He strode to a cupboard and hauled out a sack of them, setting her up with a cutting board and a knife at the counter. "Why don't you wash about five of those and cut them for stew while I grab a shower. I'm fine with skins if you are."

"You got it, boss."

Russ planted his hands on his hips and gave her a smirk, a gesture that wrinkled the corners of his eyes. "Try to not get shot at while I'm gone."

She sneered at him, pleased he wasn't being too delicate with her, and pleased his willingness to not question her extended beyond courtesy to teasing. She could use a little humor and didn't care whose expense it might be at.

She rinsed the potatoes under a trickling tap, afraid to mess with Russ's shower, not knowing if he had a well or a hot water heater or a team of oxen hauling buckets up from the creek.

She decided she liked Russ. Not just for being kind and not asking too many questions, but for the man she might've seen in him even under less dramatic circumstances. She suspected she had a crush on him as well, and the normality of such a thing felt like a miracle given the last few weeks.

Once the potatoes were cut into neat little blocks, Sarah found a huge pot under the sink and piled them inside. She dried her hands and wandered around the living area, running a palm over the hideous orange upholstery of Russ's easy chair. The couch she'd slept on had a mate, a loveseat, and both were made of deep brown leather, insanely broken in and comfy but unmistakably dated. The entire place was dated, right down to the color of the stained boards lining the walls and the homely, printed curtains. It was as though the house had gone into a coma in 1973 and never come out.

Between the kitchen and the main living area was a kind of half-wall, or a wall with its middle cut out at counter level, its sill lined with random things—colored glass bottles, a gold pocket watch, a couple of fat, dusty candles on brass pedestals. She picked up the watch, surprised by its heft. She pushed a knob and the shell popped open, revealing the clock face on one side, miniscule gears ticking behind glass on the other. She smiled sadly and set it back on the ledge.

She heard the bathroom door open but kept her attention on the kitchen, though the thought of a free peek at Russ in a towel was tempting. A minute later he appeared in clean clothes, wet hair slicked back from his face.

She smiled at him, feeling shy and wanting to hide it. She nodded to the open den. "I hate to break it to you, but this house is a bit trapped in the seventies."

"So was the previous owner."

"You're not planning to redecorate?"

"That was going to be my wife's grand project," Russ said. "But when we moved in there was more than enough that needed attention with the property alone, so it ended up at the bottom of the list. And then I never got around to doing anything. Nearest neighbors are over a mile away, so I don't usually get too many witnesses."

Russ walked to a cabinet by the couch and lifted the plastic lid off a record player. He crouched to flip through the LPs lining the shelf beneath it.

"Oh God," she teased. "Say it's not Earth Wind and Fire, to go with the decor?"

"Nope, way better. Most of these were my great-grandfather's albums." He straightened, laying a record on the turntable and setting the needle down with a crackle. Watery guitar drifted out of the speakers, ancient country music. "That's him, right there," Russ added, pointing to the framed black-and-white photo hanging above the loveseat.

Russ headed to the kitchen area as Sarah passed by to inspect the photograph. The young man looked about twenty, shared Russ's nose and eyebrows. She smiled at that. The man in that picture was younger than the one currently playing his old records, the one connected to him through two generations of yet-to-unfold romances. Her own family history was cloudy and full of holes. She envied Russ's connections to his roots.

Sarah picked up the album cover, white and blue with Hank Williams's head on a cartoon body, *Moanin' the Blues* in a chunky typeface. She grinned as Hank and Russ began to sing at the same moment, and she cast a fond, skeptical glance at her host as he gathered ingredients at the far counter. He had a nice voice, warm and mellow. He followed each and every yodely note along with the record, his head twitching this way and that.

Nice ass, she thought.

Nice man. Nice man who didn't ask questions, just tweezed buckshot out of her side and cooked her stew, hadn't laid a leering eye on her—not one she'd noticed, anyhow—and who probably had a heart too big to leave room for an ego. She'd be sad when she left here. The thought dragged her mood down, made her middle gurgle with regret and guilt.

She took a seat on the arm of the loveseat, watching Russ chop vegetables through the open wall. "Where do you get your groceries?"

He dumped a pile of carrots in the pot. "I get all my staples in town—rice and flour and all that. Everything else I get from neighbors and clients. Or from my own backyard, though I didn't get around to planting much this year. The beef you're eating tonight came from a guy whose herd I just vaccinated. Gorgeous cuts. Best job perk, hands-down."

"Cool. And do you hunt too? Or is your rifle just for scaring away stray women?"

He laughed. "I'm in no position to be scaring away any women, trust me. And the rifle's for both those things—hunting and protection. Though there's usually not too much to protect yourself from around here."

"What do you hunt?"

"That rifle there is just for pests, but I hunt deer and elk. Ducks and geese too. Rabbit sometimes."

She smirked at him, unseen. "That's very manly of you."

"Where exactly are you from?" he asked, glancing over his shoulder at her.

"East."

He didn't reply immediately, singing along for a verse before saying, "That could mean just about anywhere."

"Yeah, it could." She hoped he'd leave it there so she wouldn't have to lie to him.

"East like Minneapolis, Detroit, Boston?" Russ opened his fridge and set a hunk of red meat in a sturdy plastic bag on the counter. He waited for her answer, fixing her with a set of raised eyebrows when it didn't arrive. "Okay. We can be like that."

She pointed to the meat. "Did you know that cow?"

"Yup, though this ain't a cow." He poked the plastic. "It's a steer. And I would've given it its shots."

"Weird."

He glanced at her again, amused. "What's weird is getting your meat in a supermarket and not knowing where it came from." He turned back to his task. "Or what kind of a life it had."

"I guess."

"Happy beef tastes better. You'll see."

"You didn't even ask if I was a vegetarian," she said, teasing.

"Are you?"

"Nope. And if I was, I wrecked it with all that bacon this morning."

Russ turned fully, squinting at her. "You're a ball-buster, aren't you?"

She shrugged. "At least I don't chop them off."

He went back to work. "Well I'm rusty at impressing women with my charm and sensitivity, so keep your expectations low."

She didn't reply, just slid onto the loveseat's cushions, hoping Russ might start singing again. He did and Sarah felt sleepiness dulling her brain. She marveled at the situation she found herself in, miraculous given that only days before she'd been running out on diner checks and getting shot at by angry farmers. She thought about these records, Russ's great-grandfather's. Odd. She didn't know her *father,* period. It felt strange that people like Russ and people like her could even be living in the same decade, in the same country, welcome to vote in the same elections...let alone that they might find themselves in the same room, about to share a meal.

The last thing she was aware of before she nodded off was Russ's voice, sweet notes mimicking the scratchy record. She wondered what he sounded like other times, what it'd feel like to press her lips to his neck and make him moan. She'd just have to find out for herself.

Chapter Three

Russ set the lid on the stew and left it to its endless simmering, tidying the kitchen as quietly as he could so he wouldn't wake Nicole. Her injuries must be doing better as she'd fallen asleep flopped to one side, looking perfectly comfortable.

He turned the stereo down and cued up another of Hank's albums. He'd saved a pair of fatty, gristly hunks of meat for the dogs, and he took them outside, flung them far into the grass and made Tulah and Kit work for it. He led the horses on a few final runs around the paddock and gave the stables the nightly looking over.

Once back inside, he stopped in the middle of the den and stared at Nicole. She was damn pretty, and not simply because Russ was seven long years into his involuntary celibacy. Just plain old sexy. Bit thin, though who knew what she'd been busy doing for the last few days or weeks or months. But in any case, a lovely face, long wavy hair a couple of shades too dark to be called blonde. Those freckles and crazy honey-colored eyes.

She stirred, and Russ jumped into action, not wanting to get caught staring. He grabbed her mug off the table as if that was why he'd been there.

"Rise and shine," he said.

She yawned broadly, flashed all her teeth like a bear waking up from the winter. She glanced around, probably trying to figure out for the second time today where in the heck she was. Her gaze moved to Russ, then the stereo.

She blinked groggily through a verse then asked, "Does he ever sing about anything aside from women who done him wrong?"

"What else would a man *want* to sing about?" Russ serenaded her with the chorus as he rinsed her mug. "Stew'll be ready in an hour, I'd say. Can I get you a beer?"

"Oh, God yes." She sat up so quick Russ laughed.

He grabbed two bottles from the fridge and twisted them open, handed her one and clanked it with his own as he sank into the easy chair.

"What was that toast for?" she asked.

He thought a moment. "For you not getting lead poisoning—or worse—and for me having some company for a change."

She nodded and took a sip.

"You cold?" he asked. "I'm cold. I'll get a fire going."

"Wow, rustic."

He smiled at her, wanting to do worse. Wanting to walk over and kiss her, if only that weren't several kinds of pushy given the shape she'd arrived in. Instead he built a fire, flames crackling in the hearth in no time. He realized all these things— warm food, fire, a lazy afternoon following a morning's work, a cold drink—weren't anywhere near as enjoyable alone. A relief maybe, but not a pleasure. He took a long swallow and decided having a woman around again was like having a big mirror in the room, multiplying all the light and heat. He smiled at that, thinking even his boring old default beer tasted exciting with Nicole camped out in his den, hopefully not for the last night. If the flirting kept up, maybe once her side was healed he'd let his dick win its shouting match with his conscience and make a move on the girl.

They chitchatted while the stew simmered, its smell underscoring everything nourishing and comfortable about the atmosphere. When the laundry was done, Nicole changed into her clean clothes. She kept Russ's button-up as well, probably to hide the faded brown bloodstain on her top.

Russ got up occasionally to stoke the fire, tried now and then to get some personal information out of his guest, and failed. Instead he let her grill him about himself, about all the boring aspects of his daily life she seemed to find so exotic. He doled out two big bowls of stew and opened two more beers. They ate in the living room, she cross-legged in the easy chair, he on the couch with his heels propped on the coffee table. He had seconds and she had thirds, and once again her uncensored appetite had Russ's mind and body twitching with undignified thoughts.

Around seven, after a full hour's lazy digestion and even lazier conversation punctuated by long stretches of easy silence, Russ took away their bowls. He grabbed another pair of bottles and put a Gene Autry record on, sinking back into the couch with a satisfied sigh.

Nicole leaned forward for her beer. Perched at the edge of her seat, she took a drink then held the bottle by its neck between her knees. Her gaze was fixed on Russ's face, and the tip of her tongue teased the corner of her mouth.

He thought he knew that look...but no fucking way was he about to hit *that* jackpot. After the wait he'd had, it'd be too much to wish for. Or to fall to his knees and beg for.

Then Nicole moved, setting her beer back on the table and getting up, only to plop herself down right next to Russ. He swallowed, attention snapping between her eyes and her mouth, the small female hand on his knee.

He said something stupid, something he himself barely registered like "hello" or "what's up?" Then she put her cool, smooth palm to his neck the world dissolved.

Russ closed his eyes and brought his head down to meet hers, plunged a too-eager hand into her long, soft hair as his tongue dove between her lips, unwilling to be held back. She tasted amazing, like beer and sex and a hundred subtle female things he'd forgotten about. He cupped the back of her head and made the kiss deeper and hungrier, as dirty as the pounding erection between his legs demanded. It was demanding *more*, and the only thing that kept him from yanking her into his lap and grinding their bodies together was fear of hurting her wounded side. Instead he grabbed her thigh, tugged until she got the message and relocated herself, swinging a leg over his just how he wanted. The fire crackled and flickered in his periphery and all Russ could think was, *Christmas.*

When their mouths separated he stared down at her hips, the crotch of her jeans so tauntingly close to his. He reached around and grabbed her ass, pulled her against him. He was so hard there'd be no mistaking it through four layers of damnable fabric.

"You feel good," she muttered. Her hands stroked his chest, fingers grasping his T-shirt collar and tugging, her eager touch sliding down his back beneath the cotton, exploring. If this was pushy, Russ decided he liked pushy. He'd lost touch with this part of himself, and it was intoxicating to have a woman not just willing for him, but practically *clawing* at him. He wanted that hungry touch all over his body, those greedy hands and warm mouth, her small body beneath him, above him, buried in his covers and lodged in his chest and brain.

When her lips grazed his neck, he lost his mind.

"Lie down," he ordered, already pushing her.

He got on top, knees between hers, and he reached down to adjust himself before shoving his arms beneath her back. His mouth found hers just as he pressed his cock between her thighs, their clothes pure torture now. His hips dictated,

45

thrusting his pounding dick against her in fast, needy strokes. He felt her legs wrap around his waist, those bossy fingers digging into his shoulders. Russ's mother had warned him at length about the perils of fast women when he'd been a teenager, but for the life of him he couldn't remember a single one of those dangers now.

Her moans hummed against his lips and she pulled her mouth away. "I want you," she whispered.

"Do you?" An idiotic reply, but all he could think to say.

"Yeah. Do you have any...?"

"No."

She nodded, looking one millionth as sad as Russ felt.

"That's okay," she said. "There's plenty of other stuff to do." Her gaze flicked between his face and the miniscule space between their bodies, seeming to peruse the items from a menu of "other stuff". She tugged at the hem of his shirt, and he leaned back to peel it up and off.

Russ got lost in the pleasure, unable to do anything but watch her hands as they floated over his chest and stomach and sides then came to a halt at his belt, her fingertips so tauntingly close to his aching cock.

"Let me up?" she asked.

He got to his feet and watched her shed his work shirt and gently ease her tee and tank top off and give her bandage a quick press. If she'd planned on stripping further, Russ didn't give her the chance. He dragged her back down against the worn leather, one palm plastered to her back, the other to her breast. He brought his face in, put his nose to the space where a heavier girl would keep her cleavage and just breathed Nicole in, her sweat and skin. Miracle of miracles, he felt her touch his side, his hip, his thigh. He couldn't wait. He abandoned her breast and grabbed her hand, moving it between his legs and pressing it against his screaming cock.

"Oh God." The words erupted from his throat in a groan. It took all of his self-control to not hold her there, thrust his hips against her squeezing hand and come right here, right now.

"Tell me what you want, Russ."

He laughed, fighting for composure. He suppressed every last one of his male instincts and moved her hand down his thigh to the safety of his knee. He wasn't used to having conversations in the middle of fooling around and struggled to form an answer. "I want...I want to not wreck this before it even starts."

"I think it's already started."

He laughed again, the desperate noise trapped between paradise and hell. "Tell me what *you* want."

"I want to show you how grateful I am."

His body cooled in an instant. "Is that what this is about? About thanking me?" He held her gaze unsteadily.

"Partly, yeah. But I want this too, Russ. Trust me, it's not a favor. Or a debt."

He let go of a held breath, relieved.

"I want you to use me," she said with a smile. "But not how I'm making it sound... I want to make you feel good, to say thanks for everything you're doing for me."

"It's been ages since I've been with a woman. I could explode in about two seconds, but I miss other things way worse." His eyes and hands moved to her breasts, squeezing gently, thumbs circling the fabric of her bra until he coaxed her nipples to stiff peaks. "Let me explore you."

She nodded and Russ watched her throat twitch as she swallowed. "Let me hear you," he added, fascinated by the prospect of being with a woman who seemed likely to talk in the midst of messing around.

"Sure."

Shit, that single breathy syllable was enough to set his cock pounding again. Russ buried his mouth against her neck, tasting her skin as his hands drank their fill of her breasts. She moved against him, reaching behind to unhook her bra. He pulled the straps down her arms, probably more eager than was polite but screw it. His mouth slid downward, taking one bare brown nipple as this fingers teased the other. His free palm grazed her bandaging and he pulled away. She took his hand in hers and pressed it back over the spot, some gesture of tenderness Russ didn't fully understand but wasn't about to argue with. He felt her fingers in his hair as he suckled, her touch hungry. Sounds rose from her throat, harsh breaths and faint grunts, all of them fanning the fire blazing in his body.

He moved back. Too horny to articulate a request, he fumbled with the button of her jeans until she lay back and did it for him. She let him tug the denim down her slim legs and toss it to the floor. Russ took her in, milky pale skin, golden in the firelight. He pressed his lips to a fading bruise on the outside of her thigh, wanting to make up for whatever the world had done to her before she arrived here.

Her cotton panties were pale yellow with a pattern of tiny strawberries. Russ didn't think she could look any sexier if she had on a red lace thong and garters. He got to his knees on the couch, leaned in and kissed his way up her legs, welcomed her hand on the back of his head as he reached her inner thighs. He slid a thumb beneath the fabric at her hips, bringing his mouth and nose to her center.

"God, you smell amazing." Amazing wasn't the half of it— amazing was so far off it was a lie. There was no word for how good she smelled. Russ dug his fingers into the bit of extra flesh at her hips and brought his mouth right to her, nuzzling through the cotton. Her fingernails scraped his scalp. He took it as encouragement, pressing his tongue against her, tracing the folds he found as the cotton grew wet from one or both of them.

"Russ."

He thought he'd faint from all this—her voice, her smell, the intimate skin he could just about taste. He leaned back, yanking her panties down her legs and off her ankles. His eyes took in every inch of the new and exciting body draped on his couch, on a piece of furniture so familiar it had been invisible to him until this moment.

"Holy God." All he could do for a few seconds was stare at her, trying to commit her to memory. Then he leaned back in, brushed a hand over the curls between her thighs, light brown and soft as the hair on her head. He coaxed her legs open wide, sliding his hands beneath her ass and taking one final savoring breath before he put his mouth to her.

Soft, warm, wet...a thousand times more perfect than the imagined experience he'd have put himself to sleep jerking off over. Goddamn, he'd missed this. He prayed he was still half-good at it. Judging from the noises she made, he was just fine.

He tasted and sucked, licked and delved and got lost in her flavor and sounds, the warm, smooth skin of her thighs against his cheeks. After a couple of selfish minutes he redirected his focus, got one hand out from under her and laid it across her mound, thumb strumming her clit as he tasted her folds.

"God, Russ."

More fuel for the flames. His hips thrust softly of their own accord, and he imagined sliding inside her, feeling all this slick heat hugging his dick. Her small hand covered his, squeezing his fingers.

"Inside me, Russ."

He didn't mind taking orders. Hell, he wished girls had done that in his twenties—would've saved him a lot of hopeless guesswork. He eased two fingers inside her, thrusting shallow and slow, then deeper.

"Just like that. Suck my clit."

He smiled to himself. "Yes, ma'am."

The moan she rewarded him with was all Russ needed to convert officially to bossy-woman fandom. He took every pleading order she gave him—faster, deeper, lighter, harder. He felt powerful as her thighs began trembling, the fingers gripping his hair clenching and releasing, voice reduced to sighs and grunts and tiny whispers of the sweetest word in Creation.

"Russ."

He flicked his tongue over the hard nub of her clit, fingers thrusting fast and rough. "Come on. Come on, sweetheart."

"Russ." Then just one long moan, stilted as her hips bucked, her body giving Russ a hell of ride until she finally flopped back against the leather, ribs rising and falling under her damp skin.

He gave her one last lap of his tongue then sat up. He ran a hand across his lips and chin then regretted it—he hoped he'd keep smelling her on him for a week. He got an arm under her waist, gently hauled her to sitting and kissed her. The back of her neck was warm and sticky, and he wound her hair around his fingers, held her tight and consumed her mouth. He needed to kiss her so hard that any man who looked at her next would see Russ's brand and stay the hell away.

She pulled her lower lip from between his. "Now you. What do you want?" As she asked it her hand went between his legs, and his cock went from pulsing to pounding in a heartbeat.

"Wanna pretend we're doing it," he murmured, eyes glued to hers, too horny to be anything but crass and honest.

She nodded. Russ closed his eyes as he felt her fingers on his belt, the easy release of his buckle, the snap of his jeans, the light caress as she lowered his fly.

"Stand up a sec."

He obeyed and stood squarely before her as she tugged his jeans down his hips. He kicked them away along with his socks.

He gathered her hair in his hands again as she touched him though his underwear, a cupped palm running up and down the ridge tenting his shorts. Hypnotized, he moaned in time with her strokes.

"You feel good." She looked up and met his eyes, poured all his brain chemicals into a blender and hit purée.

Russ reached down and eased the waistband over his erection. He let her push his boxers to the floor, smooth hands torturing, sliding all the way up his legs before she touched his cock.

"Oh, God." His eyes snapped shut, all his attention centered on the pressure of her touch. The next time he peeked he saw her lips, parted, a mere taunting inch from his cock. His head was beading with excitement, so goddamn ready.

"Do it," he whispered.

That smile, pure and perfect evil. She leaned in close, close enough for him to feel her breath. She blew across his head and his dick twitched from the sensation.

"Come on. Please. Taste me, Nicole."

Her gaze darted everywhere, from his cock to his belly to his chest, to her own hand wrapped around his base giving those mean, slow strokes. The way she looked at him was thrilling. Her palm seemed to weigh him—assessing, memorizing, approving. The touch made him feel big, made him feel wanted and desired and *hungered* for. Her free fingers slid up his thigh, along his shaft to his tip, slicking the precome over his head before her mouth finally took him.

Russ gasped. "God, yes."

She sucked him, light and taunting, tongue swirling across his slit, tracing the shape of his crown. Her stroking hand tightened, the other cupping and fondling his balls for a gorgeous minute before it moved back to hold his ass, pulling him into shallow thrusts, pushing his cock just a bit deeper between her lips.

Russ let her go on for a minute, for as long as he could handle before he risked ending the evening earlier than he wanted to. He stepped back against his dick's screaming protests and released Nicole's hair to comb his fingers through his own.

"Lie down," he said though the panting.

She reclined against the leather, tongue passing over her lips in a gesture that nearly put Russ over the edge.

He got his knees between hers once more and adjusted his hips so the underside of his shaft was nestled in her wet folds. The contact made him shudder, so tempted to change the angle and ram himself inside her. Instead he lowered his body and thrust, cock sliding against her with delicious friction, as good as the real thing after seven years without it.

"Russ."

"Yeah." He watched her face, her greedy eyes. Already on the edge, his body coursed with aggression. Leaning back, he braced one foot on the floor and locked a hand behind each of her knees. He wanted to make her watch, wanted to see it himself. He stared at her face, imagining he was really inside her.

"Put your hand on top of me." He illustrated the request, grabbing her wrist and bringing her hand between them. She took the hint, wet her palm from between her legs then cupped it over Russ, his cock sandwiched between her slick hand and warm folds. The sounds she made obliterated the last of his sanity.

"Good. Good." He shut his eyes, lost himself in the sensation. Before he knew it, before he really wanted it, he was there. "Oh God. Here I come. Here I come, sweetheart."

The orgasm shook the entire length of his body, and he had to grasp her legs just to stay upright. He heard her saying his name, felt pleasure flood his cock, felt the waves of heat as he emptied on her belly. The spasms seemed to go on forever, then his whole body was glowing, floating, mind swimming, brain wiped blissfully clean. He let her legs go and lowered himself, bracing his weight on his elbows and plastering their chests and bellies together. All of this he remembered now—the smell of sex mixed with wood smoke, with dinner, with old leather and female breath. And this, tonight...this was all that and more. If Russ had to pick a moment to die, now was it. Instead he drifted closer to Earth, dropping gently back into reality as the high faded in time with the firelight.

As he came down, thoughts crept in. Vague questions swirled in his head, solidifying into worries. What did it say about Russ—what did it say about his *marriage*—that in the nearly six harmonious and affectionate years he'd been with Beth, he'd never felt anything half as potent as what he'd found in one night with the strange woman currently stroking his back? Was it Nicole, something about her? Something about him-and-her? He felt traitorous to even think it. Still, if his married life hadn't ended the way it had, would he have gone the rest of his life never feeling this? Guilt buried itself like a knife between his ribs, the pain of fearing what they'd just done had hurt Beth in its intensity...as if Russ had broken some unwritten law that said he was never allowed to get over the loss, never allowed to ask for or even to accidentally stumble onto more than he'd had with her.

Russ wasn't a worrier, though, and now wasn't the time to take it up. Besides, who knew how grandly tonight had been blown out of proportion, given the dramatic circumstances and the fact that it capped the better half of a decade's dry spell.

He swallowed and pushed up onto his palms, looking down at the face he couldn't yet call familiar.

Nicole smiled and said, "Thank you."

He laughed. "Thank *you.*"

"I need more stew now."

He returned the smile but didn't move, not quite ready to get up and let her go...but he did a minute later, grudgingly. He grabbed his boxers from the floor and cleaned them both up, tossing his shorts in the hamper and pulling on a fresh pair. Nicole was dressing as he returned to the den, and he followed suit, feeling nervous as he zipped up, feeling prematurely sober. He added a couple more logs to the waning fire.

Nicole got herself half a bowl of stew and sat, her back against the arm of the couch, bare feet tucked under Russ's thigh. The gesture let him relax again, and he put a hand on her skinny ankle, reaching for his beer with the other.

"This is really nice," she said. "Fire, food, beer, sex."

His cheeks warmed. "Yeah, it is."

"You've got every luxury a hitchhiker could ask for."

He thought he caught her gaze flash to his crotch but couldn't be sure. "I hope you'll stick around for a little bit. Not just until your side's healed. For as long as it takes you to feel like you're ready to move on." *Until you're safe, if you're not.*

"Maybe. Thanks."

Russ nodded, very suddenly overcome with desperation. He hadn't even known this woman twenty-four hours ago, yet now he was dreading her departure. Funny how the promise of sex could bring an otherwise rational man to the edge of reason. He gave her ankle a squeeze, rubbed the little knob of bone with his thumb and marveled at how small and perfect her feet seemed after all this time spent in bachelor exile among the horses and cattle and dogs.

They spoke very little, watching the fire fade as the clock neared nine-thirty. Nicole was yawning before long, but Russ was still geared up, on edge.

He gave her ankle a final squeeze. As another of her monster yawns reached its crescendo he said, "You sound like you're ready for bed."

She nodded.

"You want some shorts to sleep in?"

"That'd be nice, thanks."

He left the warmth of the den to grab her some clothes, glancing at his cold bed. She was stretching by the fire when he returned. She accepted the T-shirt and boxers, stripping and changing right in front of him.

Russ did his best to ignore his rousing cock. "Anything else you need?"

She shook her head with a smile.

"Okay... Well, I guess I'll let you get some sleep."

She smiled again, then stepped closer and laid a polite kiss on his jaw. "Thanks again. For everything."

"Sure."

She ran her fingers over his collarbone, then stepped away to begin assembling her bed for the night.

"Do you..." he began.

She looked up.

"Would you like to sleep with me? In a real bed, I mean?"

"Thanks, Russ, but this is fine. I'm sort of a restless bedmate. I wouldn't want to keep you up, tossing and turning. Especially after what I put you through last night."

"I don't mind." He quit his protests when he caught how tight her smile was. "Anyhow, invitation's open."

"Thanks." She turned back to her blankets.

"Good night, then."

Nicole didn't glance up. "Night, Russ."

He scrubbed his face in the bathroom, brushed his teeth. He clicked off the light and kept his eyes away from the den, went straight to his chilly room with its far too big bed and stripped to his underwear. For a long time Russ lay staring up at the ceiling, tugged in a hundred directions. Sleepy, anxious, horny, relieved, terrified. After perhaps half an hour he knew what he wanted, the only thing that would let him relax. He tossed his covers aside and crept out into the den. Nicole was curled on her side on the big old couch, placid face glowing in the dying firelight, hands at her heart with the blanket wadded between them. Russ took a seat at her feet and shook her calf gently until she woke.

"Hi," she mumbled.

"Hi. Can I sleep with you?"

"A little late for that, Russ."

"Sleep next to you, I mean." He was aching to add "please" but felt pathetic and needy enough already without making the begging official.

She was quiet a moment, and Russ couldn't let hesitation win, couldn't handle her refusal. He wedged himself behind her and weaseled his way into the covers, hugged her back to his chest and buried his mouth behind her ear. Her tense body relaxed after a few seconds.

"Sorry if this is pushy," he whispered.

"Pushy's eating all your host's food then making a move on him," she countered.

He laughed. "I like pushy, then." He held her tighter, until she squirmed, and he realized he must have pressed into her wound. "Sorry."

"Don't be sorry, Russ."

"I'm rusty with women."

"Could have fooled me."

"Oh...well, good. Your hair smells really nice," he added, slipping with relief back into their easy rapport from before the sex.

"It's your shampoo."

"No, it's you." He took a deep breath of her scent then regretted it, tried to focus on how comfy and sleepy he felt before his cock got other ideas.

"You smell good too." She yawned. "You smell like a man."

"That doesn't sound good."

"It's good... Where I'm from, the guys who don't smell like B.O. or cigarettes smell like cheap aftershave. Or all three. You just smell like...man."

"You sure I don't smell like horse?"

He felt her silent laugh, then another yawn. He caught it and exhaled deeply against her neck. He wanted to turn her over and kiss her until they fell asleep or started messing around again. But he resisted, unclear if he'd scored a thank-you fuck, a pity fuck or an honest-to-God I-just-wanna-fuck-you fuck. To be honest, he'd take any of those, but damn, he wanted it to be the last. He wanted Nicole to say something that echoed what he was feeling, something like, *What happened earlier was incredible. I've never felt that with someone before.* But he'd take silence. Silence beat *Oh that? Yeah, that was all right.* Better than all right to Russ, better than the best sex he'd ever had before, celibacy-bias or not. So good it'd gotten his brain stuck, tuned to this annoying, insecure frequency.

"Good night," he whispered.

"Good night, Russ. Thank you for the hot sex."

He smiled so broadly he wondered if she could feel it against her neck. He pressed his face deeper into her hair and fell asleep, probably slept half the night still wearing that shit-eating grateful grin.

Chapter Four

Russ woke to the smell of bacon. He also woke to a sight he hadn't seen in ages—the clock on the wall above the couch telling him he'd slept past seven. Nicole was across the den in the kitchen with her back to him, puttering at the stove. Another sight he hadn't been treated to in forever, a woman cooking for him. Her hair looked dark, damp.

He pushed himself up to sitting, legs tangled in the blanket. "I slept through you getting up and taking a shower?"

She turned and smiled, waving a fork at him. "Yup. Morning."

"Apparently."

"I figured if you didn't set your alarm, you probably didn't need to be anywhere."

He nodded.

She turned back to the sizzling pan. "Do you have any assignments today? Er, appointments?"

"Not on a Sunday, so long as no emergencies crop up." He kicked the covers away to stand and stretch, then realized he was once again the underdressed one. He strolled to his bedroom and pulled on jeans, donned a shirt and sweater against the morning chill. Before he could change his mind or chicken out, he strode to Nicole, put his hands on her waist from behind and kissed her neck.

"Smells good," he said, trying to keep the growl out of his voice. Woman, bacon. Hard to top that combo.

"How do you like your eggs?"

"Scrambled's fine."

"You sure? I worked at a diner in high school. I can make any kind you like. It's practically the only thing I *can* cook." She leaned over to pour him a cup of coffee.

"Thanks. Surprise me, then."

She nodded and Russ let her go. He went to the front, grabbing the newspaper off the porch and settling in with it and the coffee at the table while Nicole cooked. Not bad. Not bad at all. Then the dogs began their morning chorus, and Russ abandoned his brief spell of laziness to feed them and tend to the horses. When he got back inside, Nicole was setting plates on the table.

"Sunny-side up," she said.

"Fine by me." Russ took a seat, admired the offering.

She sighed, theatrically annoyed. "Not just *fine*. I'll have you know this like the holy grail of egg cooking. Sunny-side up with no snotty clear bits, no hard yolk?" She sat with an air of smugness and reached for the salt and pepper.

"You're a pro."

"Are you putting me to work today?" she asked.

"If you're up for it. And it seems like you've already put yourself to work." To illustrate, Russ took a bite of his toast. He looked at her face, remembering with a zap to his nerves the details of what they'd done last night. He hoped he'd keep remembering it all day long, little happy shocks like static electricity keeping him on his toes.

"I think I'm up for nearly anything now," she said. "Just not super-heavy lifting."

She smiled and ran her fingers through his messy hair, down his stubbly cheek. "Anyhow, thanks. But for now, chores. Then dinner, then who knows." She grazed a conspiring hand over his neck. "But after that I'm catching up on my beauty sleep."

Russ looked as if he was resisting the urge to turn that comment into a corny flirtation. Instead he stood and put his hand in her hair the way he seemed to love doing, leaned in and kissed her. Mouth closed, eyes closed, warm lips holding in a faint noise, a grunt or sigh.

He let her go and she stared at his chin, a little drunk from him. She reached up to wipe the yolk from beside his smiling lips.

"Okay. Put me to work."

An hour later Sarah could confirm that shampooing a horse was indeed very much like washing a car, right down to the hose she was using to rinse the suds from Mitch. She craned her neck, looking to where Russ was standing in the pen, fussing over Lizzie's gums. He'd ditched his sweater as the sun had risen, and he looked good in his dusty jeans, those strong, tanned arms, shoulder blades flexing under his T-shirt. That hat like a cliché, so endearing.

She chewed her lip, only fretting for a moment about whether or not to be evil to him. She let the hose trigger go, pumped it a couple times.

"Russ?"

He turned. "Yeah?"

"Hose is acting weird."

His eyebrows rose. He gave Lizzie a pat then left her be, walking over. "What's it doing?"

"It's just kind of—" She squeezed the handle, soaked Russ from head to toe and sent his hat flying off behind him. When she finally released it, he blinked at her, hair dripping, shirt plastered to his chest, the front side of his jeans dark and drenched.

"Seriously?" he asked.

She bit her lip. "Yeah."

Russ smiled, a deadly Jack Nicholson sort of smile, eyes narrowing. He took a step closer. "Seriously?"

She nodded.

"How fast can you run?" he asked.

"Real fast."

"You better hope so."

He took another step, and she tossed the hose aside, bolting past him into the pen and ducking between the wooden fence rails. She felt him grab her sneaker for a second, heard his feet hit the ground behind as she took off into the yard. He caught her easily after only a few seconds' sprint into the tall grass. She yelped as he hooked her around the waist and brought them both crashing to the ground, Russ taking the bulk of the impact. Rolling her onto her back, he pressed his dripping front against her and made her feel six years old, made all the horrors from the past few weeks dissolve until the entire world consisted of just their two bodies, this patch of earth under this exact sky. She began to laugh, convulsive, cathartic sobbing laughs as Russ flipped her over on top of him. She kissed him, square on the mouth with her eyes open, and decided he was the handsomest man she'd ever seen or touched or tasted.

He made the kisses deeper, dirty hands in her formerly clean hair. She locked her thighs around his hips, wanting to stay right here for a month, so filled with good feelings there was no room left for bad ones. She felt Russ grow hard and contemplated a near-literal roll in the hay, then decided the risk of ticks and every other thing lurking in the grass was a mood killer.

She let the kissing linger for another minute then freed her mouth. "You feel like a shower?"

"I feel like you just gave me one back in the paddock."

"Do you feel like a proper one, with soap and hot water and naked strangers corrupting your cramped little ancient bathtub?"

He smiled, expression shifting in a way she adored. "Yeah, I could go for that."

She got to her feet and let Russ take her dirty hand in his for the short walk back to the pen. He let Mitch out into the main yard and put away a few things and led them inside. They ditched their shoes at the door and headed for the bathroom.

Russ got the shower running and they watched one another undress. She loved his body...unlike any man's body she'd been intimate with before. Not skinny, not bulky, strong and muscular but not from the gym. Just exactly what a man ought to look like, she decided. Russ had sexy shoulders, triceps so defined she wanted to bite them. He also had the very start of what would be an inevitable middle-aged belly, a charming flaw flying in the face of his otherwise *too* perfect working man's body.

Russ shed his shorts, his sudden and complete nakedness pulling her out of her spacey admiration and into darker, curious realms. She undid her bra and let him step forward and push her panties down, his erection brushing her navel. She was about ready to trade a kidney for a box of condoms.

Strong hands took hold of her jaw, and she melted into him, into his forceful mouth and eager body, into the moans humming in his throat, begging to be unleashed. She slid her hand between them and stroked his soft chest hair, squeezed the hard swells of his shoulders. For a few greedy seconds, she explored his back and that textbook-perfect ass, then he pulled away, grinning. Sliding the shower curtain open, he gestured for her to get inside.

It wasn't the ideal tub for a tryst—narrow and rounded—but with Russ here she couldn't imagine a better place to be. He climbed in after her, dragging the clear curtain around them and angling the showerhead at her back.

"Jesus." His gaze slid up and down her front. "You're gorgeous."

She bit her tongue, tempted to contradict him. Tempted to say she'd prefer to weigh ten pounds more and be filling her modest B-cups again, lose the ribs, lose the holes in her side and the bruises that peppered her like finger-paint smudges. Instead she let him ogle, let him feast on whatever he saw and whatever made his green eyes narrow the way they did now.

She reached around the curtain for the shampoo bottle on the windowsill, snapping it open and getting her hands full of lather. Russ leaned in and let her wash his hair before he returned the favor, his fingers dawdling well after the suds had disappeared down the drain. They passed the soap back and forth and explored one another's bodies. Their curious, slippery hands lingered here and there, eyes darting as though they'd invented all this nonsense and couldn't quite comprehend their own genius.

The hot water waned. Russ stepped out first and grabbed them each a towel.

Sarah squeezed her dripping hair into the tub. "That was way more fun than shampooing a horse."

"Agreed." Russ toweled himself off then turned to the sink and lathered his face with shaving cream. He procured a razor Sarah wished she'd known about before she'd settled for his electric shaver the previous afternoon.

She sidled up him as he ran the blade down his cheek.

"May I?" she asked.

His eyebrow jumped up. "You may, if you know what you're doing."

"Sure I do." She knotted her towel between her breasts and took the razor, dragging it gently down Russ's jaw. She loved this tiny taste of trust, the proximity of his face. Selfishly, she loved every scrap of intimacy she could share with this man before their time together ended. She knew it would end badly, that it would end in such a way that neither of them would want to remember even the good parts. But for a little while longer she could live in the present—the perfection—before she wrecked it.

She maneuvered the blade down the dip between Russ's lip and chin. "Did you figure out if you have any sleeping pills?"

He pulled his head away a moment to slide open a drawer at his hip. He rummaged for a small, flat box and set it on the counter. "It's just nighttime Benadryl. Should do the trick."

"That's great, thanks." She scanned the drawer's other contents before he slid it shut. "You must have to be careful about what you leave lying around. You know, so you don't get your pills mixed up or if the dogs got ahold of something..."

Russ had a glazed look to his face, clearly distracted by other thoughts. "I'm pretty careful."

"What would happen if the dogs did get into something like this?" She tapped the box. "Would it hurt them?"

"Not that stuff. It's got the same analgesic vets prescribe for dogs."

Relief rose in her chest only to be replaced by fresh anxiety and guilt. A strong urge tugged at her, begging her to get lost in their sexual connection and block out the guilty gray clouds rolling in on the horizon.

Russ's eyes were locked on the base of her neck. As she traced a finger from his throat to his navel, she caught him swallow, his stomach swelling with a steadying breath. He braced a hand on either side of the counter. She unknotted the towel wrapped around his hips and let it fall away. His cock was ready, standing out thick and stiff from the damp nest of his dark curls. As her hand wrapped around him, he moaned as though she'd burned him. His back arched, and he leaned against the sink, hips seeking more of her touch. Russ made helplessness into the sexiest male quality she'd ever seen, and made pleasing him into the greatest act she'd ever taken part in.

She gave him long, slow, worshipful strokes. He reached for her towel, and she let him free it so he could stare as she teased his cock and made him groan and pant and sigh with pleasure. When she sensed him getting close she dropped to her knees, hand still pumping, and brought her lips to his head.

"Oh God."

"Come for me, Russ."

"God, Nicole."

She shut her eyes against the pain of hearing that name and focused on his taste.

"I'm gonna come."

She knew it was a warning, one she had no intention of heeding. His hips thrust, speeding her strokes, the fingertips of one hand set just behind her ear. For the few moments she had left, she spoiled him rotten, sucking hard, swirling her tongue over his head each time he withdrew. She took him deep as his cock shuddered, took all he gave her and moaned for him, feeling warm and content and happy as though she were the one who'd just climaxed.

Russ slumped back against the sink. "Oh God."

She swallowed, then accepted his shaky hand and let him pull her to standing. His face was flushed pink beside the white shaving cream.

She laughed softly and smiled. "You're very handsome when you're incapacitated," she said, picking up the razor.

His reply came out breathy. "Oh yeah?"

She nodded. "You're handsome when you're up to your elbows in horse shit too, but it's tough to top how you look right now." She touched his chest and ran her thumb across his bottom lip, dabbing away a fleck of white. "I better finish what I started."

Russ let her shave the rest of his chin, his expression placid, eyelids heavy with post-sex laziness.

"All done." She rinsed the razor and Russ did the same with his face. They toweled their hair and stole looks at one another's bodies. She knew her chances to enjoy this man were ticking away, going, going, gone as the sun inevitably lowered and set and the moon rose. But the longer she put off the inevitable, the harder it would be to go through with it. And the crueler it would be to Russ. She swallowed a lump of sadness as she hung her towel up and slipped back into her clothes.

"So," she said. "What's next?"

He looked up from fastening his belt. "Did you... What just happened. Can I return the favor?"

She ran a palm over her cheek. "Is my five o'clock shadow coming in?"

"You know what I mean."

"Later, Russ. I'll let you make it up to me, I promise. For now, just put me to work. Let me earn my stew." *Let me make this up to you...or start to.* Maybe in a couple of years, by some miracle, she'd be in a position to undo what she had planned for tonight. Maybe she'd be able to come back under some other name and knock on Russ's door, accept the abuse she'd have coming and tender a little restitution.

"So what's next?" she repeated, hating the faint shake in her voice, a tremble Russ wouldn't hear.

"Now I check my phone, make sure there's no surprises. Then you're helping me mend a fence. How's that sound?"

She nodded and put on a brilliant display of fake cheer, so good she nearly bought it herself. "Whatever you say, boss. Doc. Dr. Boss-man."

Russ held his hand out and she preceded him into the den. She watched him putter for a few minutes, making them a fresh pot of coffee and decanting it into a battered old metal Thermos. She studied his back, his arms, his wet hair. All these little details that added up to the kind, generous man before her, his packaging so fitting for all the beauty inside, all his trust and patience and good humor. She'd hurt people before...badly. Always with some measure of regret, but always with good reason. Not Russ. When she left here she'd do so with guilt rising behind her like dust, and for once she wouldn't be able to justify her way out of the bad memories. She only hoped she'd be able to kick up enough dirt to obliterate her trail.

Russ held the door for Nicole just as the sun dipped behind the mountains to the west...early. That time of year again. He loved fall for its smells and the colors and the blissful cool creeping into the air, but he missed the sunshine already. He missed the productivity it offered as much as he dreaded the boredom of winter. He felt the chill now and set to work prepping a fire. Nicole disappeared inside the bathroom, probably to try to lose some of the dirt and grime she'd picked up while helping Russ around the property.

Stacking the logs in the hearth brought back memories of everything from the previous evening...her body, her eager hands. God, her voice. By the time Russ had realized he could easily have dreamed up an excuse to drive to town and pick up condoms, it'd been too late. *Idiot.* But there was always tomorrow, presumably. Nicole seemed happy helping him out here and hadn't made any noises about moving on. Unless he managed to screw it all up tonight, tomorrow was another day.

She appeared from the bathroom looking tired, frayed around the edges, surely ready for a good meal and a rest. Russ diplomatically cooled his body, preparing himself for disappointment if she wanted to forgo the exertion he'd been aching for since the long kiss they'd shared after a quick lunch...after what she'd done to him in his bathroom.

"I better take it easier on you tomorrow," he said as she sank into the couch cushions. He got a record going and watched her flexing her slender feet on his coffee table, thinking that lapse in etiquette was just about the sexiest thing he'd seen in ages.

"I like working," she said, watching her wiggling toes. "My life's been chaotic for the last few weeks. It's good to have assignments to keep my brain busy, I guess." She met his eyes and smiled tightly.

Russ smiled back and studied her face in warm glow of the now-crackling fire. "How many beers you think it'll take for me to get your story out of you?"

She glanced down at where her fingernails were cleaning one another in her lap. "I'm a pretty private person."

Russ waited until she looked up again then nodded. "Understood. Well, we worked too late for me to make anything thrilling for dinner. You mind leftovers?"

"I love leftovers. Bring it on. Anything I can do to help?"

Russ shook his head. "Take it easy. Probably bad form that I've been putting my patient to work all day. You just relax."

"When do the dogs eat?" she asked.

"After the humans."

"Could I feed them, later? Maybe bring them a couple treats from the stew? I'd like to make a better impression on them than my first one."

Russ opened the fridge and hauled out the pot. "Sure. Feeding those two will definitely put you in their good graces. I'll show you where the kibble is later." Flipping on a burner, he left dinner to warm. He grabbed two beers and headed for the living area. With a sigh he sat on the coffee table, registering the day's work in his body.

Nicole accepted her bottle with a warm, tired smile and clanked it against his. "Thanks. Cheers."

"Cheers." Russ took a drink and thought it tasted sweeter than anything he could remember. Well, nearly. Beer, Roy Acuff on the turntable, fire in the hearth...yet nothing tasted, sounded or smelled better than the woman sitting in front of him. He studied her face as she did the same to the flames across the room behind Russ's back. He wondered how long she'd stay. He wondered how long he could make it before he started scheming of ways to try to get her to stay indefinitely.

"How soon 'til dinner?" she asked. A sip from her bottle hid a smirk Russ could swear he'd seen forming on those wide, mischievous lips.

"Long as you please."

"Maybe twenty minutes?" she asked, definitely smirking.

Russ nodded, waiting for her to make the move that would confirm his most selfish hopes. She set her bottle beside his butt on the table and slid forward, nestling her knees between his.

"Can I see your bedroom?"

Half the blood in Russ's body rushed south, leaving him dim-witted and pulsing with the animal urges left once the rational human in him took off. Now that he knew her intentions, he was ready to do what he hadn't last night or this morning—be the man, take the lead. He stood and let her skirt the table before he struck, hooking an arm behind her knees and hauling her into his arms.

71

She laughed and held on. "Oh my. Going caveman tonight, are we?"

"I'd never drag a lady by her hair." He walked her into his dark bedroom and nudged the dimmer up with his elbow. Tossing her bodily onto the bed, he earned a gasp and creak of springs. Russ stood before her and stripped his shirts away, dropped his jeans and toed off his socks. Nicole stared, her slow, greedy smile lighting up the dim room. Russ grabbed her elbow and pulled her to standing, dragging her top up her slender trunk and arms, and tossing it aside. He reached around to fiddle with her bra clasp and let out a low gasp of his own when her palm cupped his straining erection. Hands already shaking, he slid the straps from her shoulders. He fought to ignore memories from that morning, how she'd dropped to her knees, mouth inches from his cock, her hungry expression making promises to him just as it was now.

Russ swallowed. He clasped her wrist and moved it from his dick to his thigh. "Lie down with me?"

She sat and reclined without a word, her wide, eager eyes on him as arousing as the filthiest diatribe she could have recited. Russ lay down beside her, and they kissed for all of a minute before his hands took over. He tangled his fingers in that insanely soft hair, devoured her mouth with his lips and plunged his tongue in for deep tastes. Their bellies touched, then their hips. Russ let her feel how badly he wanted her, and prayed she wanted him back even a quarter as much. Her hands had him believing it. The scrape of her nails over his shoulder blades set Russ moaning, shifting him wholly from man to animal, from horny to ravenous. But he owed her first, from earlier. He'd make good too, pay up and earn the selfish things his body was burning for here in his bed.

"Turn over," he muttered.

She flipped onto her other side and Russ pulled her tight against him. He got her jeans open and together they managed to kick them down her legs and onto the bedspread. Russ slid an impatient hand between her thighs, met by shocking heat and a deep groan as his fingertips traced her through her underwear.

"Russ."

It was his turn to moan. He pressed his face into her hair and neck as his fingers explored. He breathed her in, memorized her. His hips pressed closer, rubbing his stiff cock against the soft flesh where her thighs met her butt. He needed more, needed it dirtier and closer, crueler.

"Take these off," he whispered and did the same to himself, pushing his boxers down his legs. When their bodies came back together, Russ thought he'd die from the pleasure, from the hot drag of his bare skin against hers. He reached down and got his cock between her thighs.

"God, Russ."

Her legs tensed around him, then released as his fingers coaxed her back open. He moved them to her lips and found her wet. Sliding two digits inside, he took them away to taste, remembering how thoroughly he'd wanted to drown in her the previous night. He put his hands back to work, getting his fingertips slick and rubbing them over her clit.

Her words came out through a gasp. "I want you."

Russ pumped his hips to thrust his cock between her legs. His head slipped against her lips with each push, the most wonderful and maddening feeling.

"I want you too." He wanted a dozen things, among them to lose his good sense and forget the existence of condoms or consequences... Hell, keep the consequences. His body wanted to get this extraordinary woman pregnant and wake up with everything he'd been wishing for the last few years, all the things that at thirty-six he'd already begun giving up on. He slid his free hand beneath her hip and held on tight, hammering his body against hers as his fingers circled her clit. He fantasized about making a miraculous mistake, angling his cock and sliding inside her, getting lost in her heat and depth and wetness.

"I want you so bad." He spoke the words against her neck and felt her second the wish as her hand reached back to squeeze his shoulder. He held his breath, waiting for permission to do the wrong thing.

"Tell me how you'd do it, if you could," she whispered.

Russ's excitement surged to drown out a flash of disappointment. "I like being on top," he murmured. His fingers stroked her faster, driven by the thrill the idea gave him.

"How do you want me?" she asked.

"On your back. I want you to watch me."

"Show me now."

Russ let her scoot away to settle against his bedspread. He knelt between her thighs, attention tugged in a hundred directions across the landscape of her body. A moan lodged itself in his throat as she lay her wrist at her belly, slim fingers taking over where Russ had left off. He fisted his cock and watched her tease her clit. What he'd said about wanting to be watched...that was true right now. He loved her eyes, and he loved how it felt when they were on him, like an invisible hand spreading warmth across his skin. Like an extra sense science didn't know about.

"You look so good," she murmured. Her gaze was on his hand and dick. "And you taste good."

Russ tightened his grip and shut his eyes, remembering that moment when she'd welcomed his release, drunk him down like wine. He opened his eyes to stare at her face. "Tell me what *you* want."

She licked her lips, and her eyes lost their focus as she thought about the question. "I love your body. I want to see you working when you take me."

That dovetailed nicely with Russ's wishes. He leaned back a fraction, coaxing her hand away to rub the tip of his erection against her clit.

She groaned, eyes clamping shut. When they opened, they were locked right on Russ's. "I want things that probably aren't all that sexy or practical in reality." She smiled up at him.

"Like what?"

"Like I want you to take me outside, take me in the grass or the dirt, or the bank of a river somewhere."

He let those ideas tumble around in his skull, finding no issue with any of them. "People got it on without beds and sheets for millennia." He swirled his cock head around her clit in tight circles. "Still do."

She smiled again. "Maybe."

"You're a long way from home, city girl." Or so he guessed. "If you want to get laid in the great outdoors, just ask me."

"There's a lot of bugs and dirt and lumpy rocks around here. I think it probably works better as a fantasy."

Russ shrugged as best he could without interrupting his hand's rhythm. "I've got nice clean blankets too."

She bit her lip. "True."

"Cool air and warm sun on your skin. Chilly water everywhere except where our bodies are touching?"

Nicole grinned, nose crinkling. "You're good at this."

"Well, you put terrible thoughts in my head." He stared between them, wanting so much more than the teasing pleasure they were sharing now. He wanted it rougher. He wanted his cock inside her slippery folds, the feel and the sound of his thighs slapping hers, the frantic greedy motions of their bodies

75

using one another. He wanted her voice begging for him over and over as he drove deep. He wanted to feel like a *man* again—not the workaholic Russ-shaped shell that'd been rattling around in this house the past few lonely years. He wanted to be twenty-nine again, the age he'd been when he'd decided to feel sorry enough for himself to stop living. And with Nicole he felt like that man. Looking down at her now, he could just about cry with gratitude.

But staring at the naked female body laid out across his bed also redoubled the lust, drove away some of Russ's sentimentality and ushered the desperate hunger back in its place. He abandoned the teasing and wedged his knees under Nicole's thighs and leaned in, hands braced at her shoulders and his cock resting against her pussy. He held there without moving, stared into her eyes and smiled.

She smiled back. "What?"

"I can't believe you're here."

Her grin deepened. "I guess single women don't come by to bother you as often as coyotes."

Russ laughed politely but held back a dozen corrections he wanted to share, knowing they were too earnest, given how new he and Nicole were to each other. She was more than just a single woman to him. A wistful part of himself that Russ hadn't been in touch with for half a lifetime thought she'd been brought here by something more meaningful than a coincidental blast of buckshot. By fate, maybe.

"Nicole," he began.

Her eyes darted between his, uncertain.

Don't scare her off now. "You're beautiful," he said, and left it at that.

She pursed her lips, moved her gaze down his torso. "You're beautiful too."

Russ shook the sentimentality from his head. He let his body take over, arms locking, hips running his cock along her wet lips like the night before...except this time he wasn't going to lose himself after a minute's frantic pleasure. Tonight he wanted to feel her come against him, as close as he could get to that thing his body was screaming for.

"God, Russ."

He shut his eyes at the sound. He let her voice drift through his body as her hands surveyed his skin, warm palms running up and down his arms and chest and sides.

"Faster."

He took the order happily. He felt a surge of sexual aggression, that desire to take, to be rough and selfish and animalistic, so long as she could handle it. The hands on his racing hips told him she could, that she wanted to uncover that side of Russ as badly as he did.

"Wanna make you come," he muttered.

"Keep going."

He leaned back on his knees, keeping the motions going as he grabbed her thighs and held them tight to his hips.

Nicole brought her hand between them and pressed it over Russ's cock. He could feel the sweet friction of her clit against his ridge each time he pushed forward, could feel her body jolting in time with it.

Russ imagined the things she'd talked about—sex under the endless blue sky, in the grass, in the water—hell, in the mud. Fall colors like now, then snow falling outside the window and a fire in the hearth, then green, green spring everywhere as his truck rattled down the never-ending dirt road toward town, Nicole in the passenger seat. He'd wandered back into his romantic haze without intending to, and he didn't stumble out again until he felt her nails raking his skin, her body begging his to keep going, to take her where she wanted to be.

He stared down at her, rapt. "Come for me."

"Russ."

He sped up his strokes, looked into her eyes, and felt powerful and helpless all at once. "Come on. Please."

Her eyes snapped shut as her back arched and a deep, harsh moan seemed to curl her body from the inside out. Her hands grasped his backside and held him still as she moved herself against his cock in small motions. Russ thought he'd catch fire from the heat of her wet lips. Blood and power thundered through his veins, and with the crazy, sentimental thoughts from earlier pushed out of his mind, he gave himself over to his body's wishes.

He relocated his knees to either side of Nicole's waist so his dick hovered above her breasts, her palms on his thighs.

"Touch me." Not quite a command, but not a plea either.

She smiled as she took the order. One hand cupped his hip as the other wrapped around his cock.

"Tighter."

Her fist squeezed him hard.

"Good. Stroke me."

The pleasure was unbelievable, a good part of it rooted in the bossiness. Russ hadn't been this way in so long, and even with Beth he'd held back. He wanted a taste of what he'd forfeited when he'd adopted the role of gentle husband.

"Be rough," he muttered.

Nicole's eyes were narrowed and heated as she gave him what he asked for—mean, fast pulls that lit him up with pleasure.

"More. Don't stop." He reached a hand out to touch her breast, a firm squeeze at first, then a gentle pinch of her nipple. Her lips parted with a harsh sigh, unmistakable pleasure. He tweaked her harder and watched with fascination as her body reacted, back arching again. He added his other hand, playing with her as the pleasure reached a violent boil deep in his belly.

Reality dissipated like steam. All Russ knew of was the tight fist stroking his cock, the soft flesh quaking under his touch, the smell of female sex and sweat, and a desperate need to release—to watch his come lash the pale skin of this glorious woman's breasts and to feel as if she were his.

"Come on, Russ." Her voice echoed just how he felt—hungry. He remembered that moment in the bathroom, a beautiful woman on her knees, thirsty for him, as though she wanted Russ more than any other thing on the planet. The image of her lips wrapped around his cock sent the last of his self-control out the window. He fumbled his way forward, knees right up around her ribs. He grasped the headboard with one hand and his dick in the other, angled his head to her mouth and jacked himself home.

He heard her mumble his name one last time as his body erupted, felt her smooth palm cup his balls and squeeze him gently as the orgasm hit.

"God, Nicole." His hips bucked with the spasms as his release streamed over his knuckles, her chin, her lips before they closed around him. "Oh, fuck."

Russ gulped steadying breaths and became aware once more of the room and its cool air, the sweat streaking his skin. He'd closed his eyes and he opened them just as Nicole swallowed. The scene knocked some sense into him, tensing him with guilt. He moved to the side, curling his body against hers and dabbing at the mess he'd made on her chin. He tried wording the apology in his head...then she touched him, mussed his damp hair and smiled.

"Awesome," she said.

He returned the smile hesitantly. "What is?"

"Just you," she said with a shrug. "When you're all worked up."

"Oh. And here I was about to apologize for being too rough. And...I dunno. Too filthy."

She laughed and pushed up onto her elbow. Staring at him, she reached out to smooth his overgrown hair and tuck it behind his ear. "Sex is supposed to be filthy. If it's not, you're probably doing it wrong."

Russ mulled the thought over, tempted to convert to her philosophy.

She traced his brow and nose and mouth with a fingertip. "You know all about animals...you must believe in them doing what's in their nature. And you're an animal too, you know."

He nodded.

"I'm an animal," she said.

"I suppose."

Nicole's brows rose. "Oh, I am, don't you worry." She flopped back against the covers with a happy sigh. "So don't ever fuck me like I'm a lady, Russ."

It was his turn to sit up. He studied her body, and the sheen of her skin, watched a vein throbbing faintly in her throat. *Animal.* The idea was exciting, like a lid lifting to reveal a treasure chest full of things Russ wanted to explore. But it scared him too. It made him wonder if he amounted to more than the nearest male in heat, and if there was room for tenderness once their two needy bodies had taken what they wanted from one another. Nicole amounted to far more than a mere body to Russ.

She reached out to touch his face again, a little taste of what Russ was needing. "The stew's not burning, is it?"

He sighed, looking around the room, reluctant for all this to end. "It could probably stand a good stirring."

They dressed in silence, and he sensed her body cooling perceptibly, the warmth of her presence waning. She tugged her long-sleeved shirt over her head. Her gaze wandered everywhere but Russ's face, and the sudden change in her terrified him. He stepped close and pulled her into a hug.

Her body was rigid for a few seconds then her arms circled his neck. "What's this for?" Her words were muffled against his shoulder.

"I'm just real glad to have you here."

"Oh." The reply was small, a glorified breath. Russ panicked again and stepped back, sensing she didn't want all this sudden affection and familiarity. He'd gotten far too good at forgetting they were strangers, far too fast. She touched his shoulder as he stepped away and offered him a sad smile.

"Better tend to the stew," he said.

Nicole nodded.

Russ led them back into the den, checked on dinner and gave the pot a good scrape.

"Can I feed the dogs while we wait?" she asked.

"Sure."

She looked into the pot. "Any nice chunks in there I could use to get into their good graces?"

Russ grabbed a mug and ladled out half a serving. "That'll do it. I'll show you where the kibble is."

"No need. You stay right here and be the pretty housewife. It's that big bag on the shelf near the door, right?"

Russ nodded.

"How much?"

"There's a can inside it, one scoop apiece. Their bowls are just by the spigot, which I know you're more than familiar with."

"Got it." She took the mug, heading for the back door. Russ watched her butt as she went then shook his head at himself.

She returned just as he was flipping the record over. She left the mug in the sink and stood by the fire while he puttered, looking lost in the flames. As Russ came by to add a log, she relocated to the couch. He dished out two bowls and grabbed a pair of dishtowels, joining her with a couple of polite feet between them on the cushions.

She took her bowl and spoon, draped the proffered towel over her lap. "Thanks, Russ."

"Sure thing." He moved the food around with his bowl but didn't eat. The air between them had grown cold and he didn't understand why. An old, ugly panic was beginning to claw at his insides—he'd lose her. Not the crippling way he'd lost Beth, but it would hurt all the same. He'd been an idiot to let his body call the shots and get him in deep with her. Who knew why she was here, but Russ bet it would blow over, and when it did she'd be wanting to get back to whatever her normal life was. It burned him that he could end up just the tiniest episode to her, a diversion, a fluke, when she'd waltzed in and overnight become the sun around which his world orbited.

They ate in silence, ten minutes that felt like an ice age.

"I guess you'll be moving on soon," Russ finally said. "Whenever things have settled down for you, back home. Wherever home is."

She turned, gaze jumping from his face to his bowl to his chest, everywhere. "Yeah, pretty soon. I can't sponge off you forever." She smiled at him, a taste of that warmth he was getting so damn attached to.

"I hope I've made it clear you're welcome to stay as long as you like."

She nodded, staring at her dinner. "You have. I appreciate it."

"It's been real nice, having company for a change. Human company."

"So you keep saying."

"And the help."

"And you've been the perfect host, Russ. When I go...it's nothing personal." She pursed her lips. "When I leave, I hope you won't think it's because I don't appreciate everything you've offered me. Or that I didn't enjoy...you know. The other things."

"You need to get home."

She huffed out a breath, nostrils flaring. "Yeah. Yeah, I need to get to home."

Russ watched her push the remains of her dinner around in its bowl. "And you need to get to bed soon too," he offered. It was early still, but he guessed she was aching for a little solitude. As much as he was aching for contact. And she probably needed rest, after what he'd put her through around the property. Idiot. He should've downplayed exactly how much work this place required.

She kept her eyes down. "Yeah. I'm getting pretty tired."

"I won't keep you." Russ stood and headed to the sink with a heavy heart. He doled the leftovers into a plastic bag and put it in the freezer beside other such bachelor-ready specimens. He filled the pot with water to soak and tossed dishes inside, dried his hands and walked to Nicole, afraid of the cold good night he felt coming. But he saw something else in her face, something softer than before. She offered a weak smile and set her bowl and napkin on the table. As she stood, Russ could see the words forming just behind her lips, perhaps a gentle suggestion that they quit with the sex, that she'd had a change of heart.

"Russ," she began.

"Yeah?"

She didn't speak. Taking a step forward, she wrapped her arms around his neck, pressed her face into the skin below his ear. He let his own arms circle her back and held her without understanding what this embrace was all about.

Her words warmed his neck. "Thank you."

"Oh. Sure."

"You've been really kind to me. I appreciate it." She stepped back and smiled deeper, sadness still clinging to the corners of her lips. "You're a very nice man. And you're very handsome."

Russ felt his cheeks warm and grinned down at his bare feet. "Thanks." He met her eyes again, struggling to keep the earnestness reined in and match the hold she seemed to have over her emotions. "You're beautiful. And you're welcome. Anytime, and for as long as you want, you're welcome."

"Thanks." She began gathering up the bedding.

"I'll see you in the morning." Russ bit back a pathetic urge to ask her to change her mind, to sleep in his bed, choked it down. "Sweet dreams, Nicole."

Another tight smile. "Night, Russ."

Chapter Five

After two hours' reading and another of tossing and turning, waiting for sleep to arrive, Russ finally nodded off. He slept poorly, had a strange dream about owls and a secret tunnel under his stable. When his eyes opened he didn't even have to look at the clock to know it wasn't anywhere close to morning—just past midnight, the digits confirmed. He sighed to himself, staring up into the dark.

His body felt itchy, an unreachable restlessness far below the skin. It was a stupid thing to think after just two days, but he felt amputated with Nicole lying so far away. He remembered his great uncle's story about getting Phantom Limb Syndrome after he'd lost his leg in Korea. Russ felt that now—a vague, ghostly presence in his bed, near his chest, right where Nicole ought to be.

He wanted to see her. He'd be good, not intrude on her as he had the second night, but he just wanted to *look* at her. Easing his bedroom door open he stole into the den, thinking he'd get a glass of water so as not to appear creepy if she woke to find him sneaking around in the near dark. He padded across the floor, searching for her outline in the moonlight slanting through the windows. Blankets, pillows, no girl. He went back a few paces, peering into the empty bathroom. Russ frowned and flipped on the lights, and where Nicole ought to be sat a heap of empty bedding. His heart thumped. Rushing back to his bedroom, he yanked jeans up his legs, socks, a T-shirt. He'd look an idiot running out into the yard only to find her there, staring up at the moon or stars, maybe crying, maybe wanting some space from him...but no. That didn't feel right. Russ hurried out the back door and pulled his boots on, waiting for the predictable ruckus.

"Kit? Tulah?"

Nothing.

He found them in their usual sleeping spots just inside the stable and fell to his knees beside Tulah. She was warm, ribs rising and falling slow and steady, but she didn't rouse when Russ gave her a good shake. Kit was friskier—she raised her head to gaze at Russ, but looked dozy.

He stood, staring out across the moonlit fields and feeling his entire world flip-flop, anger and shock rushing in to drive out the fear. "Fuck me. Bitch drugged my dogs."

Made finding her a hell of a lot harder.

His heart hammered, too many questions and actions tugging him in different directions. Those pills didn't have aspirin in them...did they? "Fuck."

Russ ran around to the front, eyed his truck but knew it was a bad idea. Even without headlights, she'd hear him coming a mile away and find a million places to hide. He toyed with calling the sheriff but the clock was ticking. And besides, she'd fucked with his dogs and that made this goddamn personal. He just had to hope he could outrun her and pray he picked the right direction to head. As he charged inside, he glanced at his rifle then thought better of it. Instead he grabbed the little pistol from his medical case and laced up his boots. He dashed back down the front steps and chose east, the opposite way she'd come from when she first arrived.

He set off at a jog. Adrenaline begged him to sprint but he needed to be the calm one, the quiet one. He was damn lucky the moon was as full as it was, the sky near cloudless.

What felt like five miles onward, he thanked God for another thing—her cream-colored shirt. It glowed in the distance, the flag of her hair flapping against it with her steps. Russ ran as fast as he could, noisiness be damned, close enough now to outrun her.

He saw her pale face as she turned, maybe fifty yards down the dirt road.

"Stop!" he bellowed, pulling the pistol from his pocket to show her.

She immediately broke into a run but kept to the road. She didn't head into the fields until it was way too late and Russ was only a few breaths behind. He tackled her, hard, sending them both rolling across the ground, flattening the already harvested wheat stalks.

She gasped and coughed, the sound of wind being knocked out. Russ scrambled for the plastic bag near her hand. It rustled as he stood.

He yanked her to standing by her waist, wounds be damned. He gripped her arm tight. "What'd you do to my dogs?"

"I g-gave them those p-pills," she gasped, still winded.

"How much?" When she didn't answer he dropped the bag, grabbed her other arm and shook her. "How much?"

"As much as the directions said to give a ch-child. Not that much."

He took a few breaths, staring at her frightened face in the bluish moonlight and hating how the relief dulled his anger. "You have any *fucking* clue how lucky you are? You could have killed my dogs."

"I wasn't trying to."

He wanted to yell at her but didn't even know where to start. Instead he let her go. He grabbed the bag and began marching her back down the road with the barrel of the gun at the small of her back, brisk enough to have her panting within a minute. The return journey felt far shorter than the way out, less than two miles. They passed the half hour in a silence punctuated by heavy breaths and soft grunts, each tripping, each tired. He led her around the rear of the house to the stable. He flipped the light on and gave her a blazing look.

"Don't you fucking think about running."

She held his stare and her tongue.

Russ stuffed the pistol into his jeans. "Where's the box those pills came from?"

After a pause she pointed to a high shelf. Russ snatched the package, and as he read through the ingredients, his heart slowed. Diphenhydramine. No aspirin. Nothing he hadn't prescribed himself for sedation or allergy treatment. He gave the dogs a good checking over and decided they'd be fine in a few hours, if a bit dim-witted.

Without looking at Nicole's face, he shut off the light and grabbed her wrist to lead her around to the front. He yanked her up the porch steps, jerking the door open and pushing her inside, nearly hard enough to send her to the floor. He didn't want to hurt her, but goddamn if he didn't want her to believe him capable of it. Believe herself deserving of it. She stumbled and recovered then turned to face him, unmistakably scared behind her steely façade.

He held her eyes as he walked to the dining area. He overturned the plastic bag on the table and out tumbled his great-grandfather's watch along with some food and a small wad of bills, ones Russ knew damn well used to be in the mint box he kept on this counter. He held up the watch as though he meant to hypnotize her.

"You robbed me? Seriously?"

She didn't reply, gaze on the watch as though he might hurl it at her, which he frankly couldn't put past himself just now.

"You a drug addict?"

Her brows bunched, unmistakably insulted. "No."

"Doesn't strike me as your taste, so forgive me if I can only assume you planned to sell it. And in a goddamn hurry."

She pursed her lips.

"Exactly how much were you hoping to get for it?" He set it down, not waiting for an answer. "Why not steal my horse tranquilizers, while you were at it? You could make a hell of a lot more off ketamine than antiques."

She stood up a bit straighter, eyes narrowing. "I wouldn't do that."

"Oh, and don't you look holy for a woman who just drugged my dogs?"

"I don't have the luxury of putting strangers ahead of myself right now."

"Poor baby. What about me then? Where do I rank on your list of people to fuck over? Where does 'sucker' rank?" His heart was pounding harder than he could remember, so hard it scared him. So hard he didn't know which might win, rational thought or blind anger.

"I'm sorry," she said quietly, staring at the floor between them.

Russ took a deep breath and slapped his palm to the tabletop. "Why didn't you steal my truck?"

She smiled tightly, nearly blushing. "I couldn't find the keys."

"They're in the ignition." He squinted at her, some of his boiling anger cooling as the adrenaline wore off. He took a few deep breaths then stepped close, closer, forcing her to back up until her calves bumped the couch. He gave her a push that landed her butt firmly on the cushions.

"Who are you?"

She stared up at his face, her eyes tired and glassy, not really connecting with his. "I thought you believed in places where people don't have to answer to others."

"That's before you drugged my dogs and tried to rob me. Who are you? Lemme see your ID."

She switched gears, pointing at the pistol in his pocket. "How close did you come to actually shooting me?"

"It's a tranquilizer gun." He pulled it out, aimed it to the side and clicked the trigger a couple of times. "And it's not loaded, since some of us have some sense in our skulls. Gimme your ID."

Her nostrils flared but she dug in her back pocket and pulled out a wallet. She handed him an Iowa driver's license. Nicole Brevin, thirty-two as she'd claimed, but this wasn't the woman on Russ's couch. All they had in common was white skin and brown hair.

He flicked the card into her lap. "What's your real name?"

She kept her eyes on his, the defiance undermined by her pursed and unsteady lips.

"Just tell me," he said. "You're already busted. And believe me, you're not escaping a second time. You already used up your best tricks and look where they got you."

She held his stare, face cold again.

"Come on, now. Just your first name. Don't act like you don't owe me that."

She licked her lips, gaze moving past Russ's leg to the floor. For once he decided avoiding eye contact was a sign of truthfulness. And hell, she'd lied plenty already, right to his face.

"Sarah," she muttered.

"Right. And how old are you actually, Sarah?"

"Twenty-seven."

He nodded. That old intuition his wife had always said men were useless with...his was waggling a big I-told-you-so finger at him. "So who's this Nicole you're claiming to be?"

She shrugged, still avoiding his eyes. "Some woman whose purse I stole at a bar."

He shook his head and tried to clear the disbelief. "Jesus... What'd you do, Sarah? Who're you running from?"

"I'm not going to tell you."

"Did you steal something? Did you hurt somebody? Is somebody trying to hurt *you*?"

Her expression changed. She was surprised by that last question—surprised by its concern. He bet she wasn't used to being worried about, but he also bet she wasn't on the run as a victim... She'd have gone to the police, presumably, instead of trying to change her identity. A totally different breed of desperate woman, this one was.

"I hurt somebody," she finally said. "But he had it coming. And I didn't mean to hurt him as bad as I did." Her voice trickled to a whisper.

"Right." The anger and suspicion and distrust in Russ's chest deflated, leaving him plain old exhausted. He stood and strode to his junk cabinet, pulling out a loop of clothesline. Sarah's eyes widened as he walked over. She stood.

Russ shook his head. "I'm so frigging tired right now, you really have no idea. Just cut me a goddamn break and cooperate."

Her shoulders slumped. "Fine."

"Turn around."

She shuffled in place and let Russ tie her wrists together, not so tight she couldn't reach the knot and maybe undo it, loose enough that she could shift her arms a little. He planned on keeping her troublemaking hands where he'd feel them, so no matter if the knots weren't ideal. He tucked the excess line into the back pocket of her pants.

"C'mon," he said, waving a hand toward his bedroom.

She made a face, incredulity mixed with a touch of disgust.

"Save your indignation, sweetheart. I haven't got anything planned you didn't already trick me into."

He caught her cheeks color as she turned to obey, walking to his room and awaiting further instructions.

"Go on," he said. "Shoes off and lie down. On your side."

"Can't we do this some other way? My hands are going to fall asleep."

"You're breaking my heart."

"Couldn't you take my clothes or something? What am I going to do, run off in my underwear?"

"You might try and smother me with a pillow," he said.

"I can't overpower you, Russ."

He hated how his brain skipped when she said his name. The last time she'd said it in this room it had meant something, something wondrous. Ruined beyond all recognition now.

"Come on, please. I'll be shifting all night if you keep me tied up."

He shook his head, too tired to argue. He twirled his finger and she obeyed, turning her back to him.

"You try *any*thing," he said, tugging at the knot, "and I swear I'm locking you in a dog crate."

"I won't."

The rope fell away and she flexed her hands.

"Clothes off, like you said."

She shrugged. "It's not like you haven't seen it all already."

Russ squinted at his covers, hating the way she'd said that. A low blow aimed right as his balls, muttered as though what they'd done had been no big deal, inconsequential, when for him it had felt like lightning striking—like finding a pot of gold buried in his backyard. Too good to be true.

She pushed her sneakers off and stripped to her underwear, didn't stir a thing in Russ except more irritation. He shoved her clothes between the mattress and the bedframe where she'd never get them unless she managed to put him out of commission. And if she did... Well fuck it then. Maybe she deserved to get away. Might make everything way easier. He was too tired to care now, too tempted by the idea of never having to look at her again.

She got into bed facing the wall. Russ sat on the edge of the mattress and unlaced his boots, feeling about a thousand years old. Still fully dressed, he got under the covers. He spooned himself behind her, low, with his face at her neck and his crotch behind her thighs. He wrapped his arms around her waist and felt her body stiffen.

"It's a big bed," she muttered.

"Don't flatter yourself. Trust me, there's nobody I'd rather be a million miles away from right now than you."

He heard her huff out a breath and huffed one right back. *A big bed,* he thought. *Too big.* A constant reminder of how alone he'd been these last seven years.

"You're turning me in tomorrow," she said quietly.

He spoke against her shoulder. "Of course I am."

"Please don't."

He sighed, trying to ignore the smell of her sweat and the impulse to run his tongue over her skin. He'd forgotten how a good fight got his blood pumping, but he still wanted to wring her neck ten times worse than he wanted to bang her brains out. Plus the sex... The sex hadn't meant anything. Just a ploy to get Russ sympathetic. Which he'd been to start with. That boiled him—she'd screwed with his heart when she knew damn well she didn't need to.

"Please."

Russ adjusted his shoulders, gave his pillow a couple whacks. "I don't have any choice. You messed with my dogs, you stole from me, did something to make one of my neighbors shoot at you..." *You fucked with my heart and gave me hope.* "You haven't done a thing to earn my pity, sweetheart."

Chapter Six

Sarah didn't escape. She didn't try, didn't budge an inch through the night. Russ woke after a couple of restless hours' sleep with a headache and an undiplomatic hard-on pressed against her warm backside. He pulled away, hoping she'd slept through his body's traitorous advances.

Russ got about twenty seconds' peace, long enough to stretch one side of his body and contemplate how to wake his prisoner. A shake? A poke? A gruff order? Then his phone beeped on the dresser, too early in the morning to be anything good.

He left the bed and pushed the Talk button. "Russ Gray."

"Russ, it's Jim from Holloway."

"Of course. Morning, Jim." Russ met Sarah's half-mast eyes in a brief warning before he wandered to the kitchen to grab a pad and pen. The folks at the Holloway dairy farm had a sick cow, and Russ hung up with a promise to swing by in the next hour. He returned to the bedroom threshold as Sarah was pulling her tank top down her torso, facing away. There was a bruise on her arm where he'd grabbed her the night before, the purple fingermarks filling him with shame. She may well have earned his aggression, but he hated this evidence he'd deemed her worth getting that upset over.

He glanced around, seeking an escape...not from the room, but from this situation. The last time he'd been badly hurt, when the universe had seen fit to take his wife away, he'd gotten lost in a bottle for a long time. Russ couldn't stand the taste of liquor now. It brought back memories of the four or five months he'd wasted being a coward, drowning in self-pity and dulled pain, putting off the mourning but not lessening it a jot. What he felt right now, staring at Sarah's back with hurt churning in his gut, acid burning in his throat... Well it felt damn close to a hangover. And now he thought about it, her eyes sure looked a damn lot like whiskey.

She pulled her second shirt on, turned and started to find him watching. "Morning," she mumbled.

"We're heading out now. I have to swing by and do a job on the way to town, and you'll have to come with me. You aren't leaving my sight, understand?"

She shrugged and those eyes he'd seen lit up in his direction only twelve hours earlier seemed lifeless now, cold and dull. "Fine. Can I at least pee without an armed guard?"

Russ nodded and let her pass him to close herself in the bathroom. He could see the outside of the bathroom window from the den, and he kept his attention glued to it until she reemerged.

"Are we eating before we leave?" She trailed a hand over his dining room table. Russ fought off an urge to slap it away, to demand to know exactly where she found the gall to touch his things or think she deserved feeding.

"They'll give you something at the station," he said coldly, and grabbed his medical case from the counter and ushered her out the front door. He locked up behind them and led to her to the truck, slammed the passenger door as she sat down and jogged to his side. He set his case behind the seat and slid the key from the ignition. "Stay here."

He headed around back to check the dogs. Kit stood as he rounded the corner, looking dim but happy. Tulah was off at the edge of the field, entranced by something in the distance.

He crouched to rub Kit's head and kiss her between the ears before heading back to the truck.

He climbed in and started the engine. "Buckle up."

Sarah did. "What sort of job are you going on?"

Russ paused, glared at the speedometer before lowering his forehead to the steering wheel. He let a long, toxic breath ooze from his chest and sat back in his seat. Turning to Sarah, he ignored the little sparks zapping his body—false familiarity, false attraction, false affection. All lies. He held her eyes for a moment, long enough to force himself to feel nothing but resignation. "I got no reason to talk to you."

She swallowed, her gaze dropping to her hands. Russ immediately inventoried the surrounding area for an object she might want to bludgeon him with and reached beneath her seat for the ice scraper. He tossed it back into his side of the cab.

"I'm not going to hurt you, Russ."

Too late. "I wouldn't put it past you."

"You're stronger than me. You're faster than me. The law's on your side. I'm desperate, Russ, but I'm not stupid."

He put the truck in reverse, as though he might be able to speed away from here and escape the sound of his name in her voice and the longing it triggered, the embarrassment he felt to have ever thought it meant something. He turned the car onto the road.

"I won't run," she said. "I'll ask you again...please don't turn me in, Russ."

"Quit calling me that." He kept his eyes on the horizon, chest aching.

"Sorry." She fell silent for a few minutes then spoke as they passed the border of Russ's property. "If you let me go, I'll make it up to you. I don't know when, but I'll send you money for everything you gave me..."

Russ's simmering blood rushed to a boil.

"...the food—"

"Shut up." He banged a fist on the dashboard, still staring straight ahead. "I don't give a good goddamn about money."

Her hands rubbed her thighs in Russ's periphery. "I don't know how else to try and make it up to you."

"You make it up to me by getting the hell out of my life, that's how."

The temperature in the cab cooled perceptibly. "Fine."

Russ sighed, the exhalation harsh and mean, not calming.

"I'm sorry," she muttered.

"Sorry you got caught."

"No, I'm sorry I hurt you."

Russ rankled and tried to keep it hidden. "You didn't hurt me. You just pissed me the fuck off." They hit a patch of bad road, truck rattling over gravel for a half mile.

"You didn't deserve to get jerked around by me," she said, voice warbling with the bumps.

"You don't say."

"I wouldn't have done it if I wasn't really, truly screwed."

What about me? Would you have done me if you weren't really and truly screwed?

Sarah went quiet and Russ felt her change. She gave up bargaining with him and her posture slumped, broken. She leaned against the window as the wheat fields streamed by. To think Russ had been fantasizing about such a thing just the previous day—this face and body he'd already gotten attached to, beside him on such a journey. Well, a damn different journey here in reality. He'd imagined driving her into town, taking her for a beer at the bar and, yeah, showing her off to the people he knew. Instead, the sheriff's station. He swore under his breath and turned the truck down the long drive toward the Holloway farm.

"Stay there," he said as he parked. He switched off the engine and walked around to her side. He opened the door and took her hand. After grabbing his case he led her to the massive metal barn's entrance, dropping her hand as Jim Ellis appeared in the threshold.

"Walk ahead of me," Russ muttered to Sarah.

She cast him an annoyed glance and did as he ordered.

Russ nodded to Jim, the farm's weekday manager. "Morning."

"Morning, Russ. Thanks for coming so quick." Jim turned his smile on Sarah, lifting his baseball cap from his thinning gray hair.

"This is Sarah. She's been helping me the last couple days. Thinking about going into equine medicine." Easier to lie than explain.

She put out her hand to accept Jim's shake.

Jim grinned deeper, clearly intrigued. "Nice to meet you, Sarah. Any particular area of interest or—"

"We better take a look at that cow," Russ cut in, sharing a panicky glance with Sarah, their first taste of unity since her disappearing act.

"Sure." Jim led them into the vast barn past rows of cows hooked up to milking machinery. They walked to the far end to a separate paddock where the animal in question stood motionless. "I wouldn't normally call you over like this, but it just hit her so fast. She looked fine last night. Now..."

Russ nodded, coming close to study the cow's streaming nostrils and glassy eyes.

"It's nothing I ain't seen before, but then I said that last winter about one of our girls, and she up and died, overnight," Jim said.

Russ nodded. "I remember. Better safe than sorry. You can go ahead and carry on with your work. I'll see if I can get you a diagnosis."

"You holler if you got questions." Jim headed back to tend to the farm's operations.

Some kind of flu, Russ guessed. He turned the cow's head this way and that, assessing her symptoms and the nasty color of its discharge. Infection, but not a terrible one, he decided. It was a relief to have this distraction, to let Sarah's presence by his side slip lower on his list of worries. He got his case open and took out a small vacuum and found an outlet for it, pulled a hose over from the corner. He disinfected the vacuum's long probe and set to work clearing the cow's nasal passages so she could breathe easier. He took a sample to have checked later for any serious signs of trouble.

Behind Russ's shoulder, Sarah cleared her throat. "Can I help with anything?"

He opened his mouth, poised to be gruff, then he turned and caught the look in her eyes—pure, agendaless concern. "No, it's fine. Or actually..." He paused his task, crouching to wet a fresh cloth with water and handing it to her. "You can wipe that crusty stuff around her eyes. Just be gentle."

"I will."

Russ watched her as the little vacuum did its job and saw how the task calmed her. He'd seen that fleeting, placid quality in her before, the times she'd helped him around his place. He didn't know what she'd been through before she'd turned up on his doorstep, but it was something that made her crave an assignment, a distraction. He knew that desire well, himself. Productivity was still his drug of choice years after he'd swapped a bottle for it.

"That's a nice job you're doing," he said softly.

She kept her gaze on the cloth. "What's wrong with her? Anything serious?"

"Bit of an infection is all, far as I can tell, though I'll want to rule out anything exotic. She'll be fine once she can breathe a little better and I get some antibiotics into her."

Sarah nodded, patting the cow's neck. "What's her name? Do you know?"

Russ craned his neck to check the number branded to her flank. "One-two-six-two-oh-two."

"Oh." Her lips quirked to a frown. "How depressing."

"You can name her something else, if you want," Russ offered.

Those honey-colored eyes met his. "Why? Because I'm so good at making up names?" There was no combat behind the words, merely sadness...apology with only the slightest bitter edge to it.

"Nope. Just thought you might want to."

She looked back to the patient, giving the tuft of hair on the cow's head a combing with her fingers. "Nah. She'd never know the difference, anyhow."

Russ wondered if Sarah had the same vision he did then—her own number stenciled onto a prison uniform, if that's what the future held for her. Strange. Russ had always had a subconscious idea of what a criminal looked like, and it wasn't this woman. This *girl*. Twenty-seven and possibly about to have her life taken away, reduced to a string of digits, perhaps another sort of label—*burglar,* maybe. But no...something worse, he bet. Something worth running from.

He finished with the vacuum, gave the cow an injection and counted out pills into a bottle for Jim to administer later. Russ and Sarah found him tending to some machinery.

"How's she lookin', doc?"

"I'm near positive it's a sinus infection, but I'll send a sample to the lab this afternoon, to be safe. I'm sure she'll be okay, though. Should perk up by tomorrow. Keep her on her own for a couple days, and give her one of these every night and every morning 'til they're gone." He handed over the pill bottle.

"Will do. Thanks for coming so quick."

"Not a problem. We were headed into town anyhow. You call me straightaway if she gets any worse." Russ shook Jim's hand and Sarah followed suit.

"Good luck with your studies, young lady." Jim tipped his brim again. He dug in his pocket and came out with a business card. "You ever get sick of horses and have any questions about the dairy business, you give me a call."

She studied the card and tucked it in her jeans. "Thanks."

They tendered their goodbyes and Russ led Sarah into the bright fall sunshine. Without speaking they climbed into the truck and Russ got them back on track, just fifteen miles between here and the end of the road. The end of Sarah's road, anyhow, the end of Russ's worry. He'd be able to draw a line under this whole debacle and get busy forgetting it'd ever happened.

"You know," he said as they neared the town line, "I hope things go okay for you. You know, as okay as possible, given whatever it is you've done."

She nodded, her focus on the horizon.

"No harm no foul, about my stuff. Or the dogs."

"Sure."

Russ's chest tightened, a feeling he couldn't quite identify clenching his heart. Some kind of sadness. Sad he'd gotten his hopes up only to have them dashed, sad for this woman stuck in the situation she was, sad for what her future held. Sad for his own future, back to how it'd looked just a few days before— steady and busy, yet empty. The truck trundled off the gravel and onto faded, cracked pavement, civilization. He drove them down the main street and into the parking lot of the little gray building where he and Sarah would become the stuff of each other's memories.

Russ killed the engine and held the steering wheel, staring out over the lot, past the town, up toward the mountains.

"So this is it, huh?" she asked.

He kept his attention on the distant hills, wishing his heart were there with it.

"Russ..."

He shut his eyes tight for a second then opened them and met her light brown ones.

"Please, Russ. Let me go."

What he saw and heard in her broke his heart—not a trace of manipulation, barely even desperation. Just fear and regret. He felt it in his own body, way down deep in his bones.

"If I let you go, it's my fault the next time you rob somebody."

She didn't deny that she might indeed do such a thing...no denials or promises to straighten up. She really didn't see another option for herself, and that about ripped Russ to shreds. He studied her face, took a deep breath to try to quell the ache in his chest.

"How come you didn't ask me for money?" he asked. "How come you thought drugging my dogs and stealing from me was the best thing you could do?"

She aimed her eyes lower as she thought about it, staring at Russ's throat or collar. "If I'd asked you and you'd said yes, I'd have owed you an explanation."

"And you don't feel like you owe me one now?"

She smiled sadly. "Probably. But also, you're a very nice man."

"You got some policy against stealing from assholes?"

She bit her lip. "I thought if I got away, you weren't the type who'd hold a grudge. I thought maybe you'd let me go, realize I'd only do that to you if I was in really deep trouble. I hoped maybe you wouldn't report it." She offered another weak smile, looking unimpressed with her own reasoning.

Russ wondered if she'd gotten him pegged about right. He couldn't be sure, given how things had ultimately played out. "I'd have lent you money. I'd have *given* you money. No questions asked."

Her eyes shifted unsteadily between his. "Would you?"

"Sure."

"Why?"

"Because I liked you. Or I liked Nicole, anyhow. I liked who I thought you were."

She drew a long breath through her nose and stared out the window past Russ. "I'm sorry I'm not her."

He swallowed, choking down a clot of painful emotion. Oddly, he missed Nicole. He'd fallen half in love with a woman who didn't exist, and now she was gone, like a dream. "It's a real shame how all this turned out."

She nodded.

"You got anything else to say to me before we go in there?"

"I already asked you to let me go, Russ. I'm not going to beg."

"Fine."

"Is there something else *you* wanted to ask me before we go in there?"

He let the steering wheel go, slid his keys from the ignition and held them tight, metal biting skin. He turned to her. "Why'd you sleep with me?"

Her eyes widened. "Why'd I sleep with you?"

"Was it to get me all cozy, lower my defenses?"

Her mouth dropped open, and she touched her lips, looking as though he'd slapped her across the face. "No, Russ. I slept with you because I wanted to. It was selfish, but I wasn't... I didn't fake any of that. I wanted that. I wanted *you.*" She looked down at her hands. "If I hadn't messed all this up and wrecked the memories for the both of us, I'd still want you, right now." She glanced up again. "You're the kindest, most genuine man I've ever met."

Russ frowned, unwilling to believe her and put himself in a position to be the dupe again.

"And I knew when we slept together I didn't deserve you, because I already knew I'd end up hurting you. But I still wanted you. I just wanted a night or two with somebody like you, because I'm not going to meet a man like you again. That's a fact. I took that, like I took your watch, knowing I didn't deserve it. And I'm sorry. Not because I got caught, either. I'm just sorry."

"It wasn't like my goddamn watch," Russ said. "You took my watch and it burns me, you know." He rubbed at the knot forming beneath his ribs. "You sleep with me, let me think maybe there was something there that wasn't...that just rips my fucking heart out. Don't compare the two. It pisses me off." Hope versus gold; Russ knew which it hurt more to lose, and which one would be keeping him up nights.

He watched her collect her thoughts. Her hands rested on her thighs, one finger picking at a rip in her jeans. "I'm the last person who's earned a chance to defend themselves, but I wouldn't have done that if I hadn't felt something too. I swear." She tilted her chin up to meet his eyes. "I just wanted to know you, while I had the chance." She looked away and Russ could see a tic in her jaw from the effort she was making to not cry. A tendon rose along her throat as deep pink patches blossomed on her neck. She was a good actress, but Russ doubted even this girl could fake herself a case of hives.

She waved a hand at the station. "Let's just go." Tears formed and fell, and she dragged her knuckles beneath her eyes, as though angry at her glands for betraying her.

"You can get yourself calmed down first," Russ offered.

"I've taken enough from you already. Don't let me waste any more of your day." She unstrapped her belt. Russ grabbed her wrist as she reached for the handle.

She tried to tug her arm from his grip. "I'm not running."

"I know you're not. Just wait a second."

More tears came, and it was the crying Russ suspected she was eager to flee from, not him. "You got family? Somebody who's missing you?"

She shook her head, wiping her nose with her free hand.

"The man you said you hurt, more than you meant to," Russ said. "Did he hurt you first?"

The words came out through a stifled sob, sticky and thick. "No. But he hurt a friend of mine."

Russ felt two bad decisions tugging him in opposite directions. He opened his mouth to speak just as the door to the station swung open. The sheriff's deputy strolled out, pulling a pack of cigarettes from his pocket. He grinned in their direction and crossed the pavement. Russ let Sarah's wrist go and rolled down his window, heart thumping against his ribs. He offered a broad smile. "Mornin', Ben."

"Mornin' yourself, Doctor. Anything I can help you with?" Ben leaned his bony elbows on Russ's window, ducking to smile at Sarah. Russ stole a glance at her, saw fear plastered all over her grinning face. He wondered if Ben was taking in her hives, her brimming eyes, maybe just her breasts... Russ tried to pick the right words, to figure out what he was supposed to do. One mental image of Ben leading her into a holding cell and the nausea it triggered was all the answer he needed.

"Oh, no," he said. "Me and my friend were just arguing about where to grab some breakfast." He smiled at Ben again, wondering what Sarah's face must be doing behind his back. "Sorry to compromise the station parking lot while we're deciding."

"Tough call," Ben said, eyes still locked over Russ's shoulder. "Diner's got the best eggs, but the café's got better coffee."

Russ nodded. "Think we'll go to the diner then. Anyhow, I'll let you get back to work."

Ben finally straightened, sliding a cigarette from his pack and wandering to the sidewalk to stare down the quiet road.

Russ jammed the key back in the ignition and started the truck. "Buckle up."

Sarah turned her head so fast it whipped her hair around. "Why?"

"Because I'm not sure what to do yet. We're going back to the house."

"Seriously?"

"I didn't say I'm letting you go," Russ said. "But I don't know what to do with you yet. Don't get your hopes up. Consider yourself under citizen's house arrest 'til I've made up my mind."

She buckled her belt and squared her shoulders. Russ could see her thick outer shell falling back into place, the pink blotches on her neck the only evidence still undermining her otherwise convincing tough-cookie act.

As he swung the truck out onto the street, Russ wondered if she'd won...if all this with the tears and the flattery had been an act he'd gobbled right up, idiot that he was. He didn't think so. His blinders were off, gone along with the mind-clouding lust. Gone was the gullible, horny romanticism, replaced by Russ's usual good-natured pragmatism.

"How much were you hoping to sell my watch for?" he asked.

She eyed him distrustfully, holding back her answer.

"Enough to buy a ticket to Calgary or someplace?"

"I can't leave the country. I don't have my passport, and even if I did it might be flagged."

"So what then?"

She shrugged. "I dunno, Russ. Just keep moving."

"For how long?"

Another shrug. "I don't think there's a statute of limitation for what I did, so forever, I guess."

Russ's people-reading faculties had indeed returned to him, and he could sense a breakdown brewing behind her blasé act. He decided to let her keep her charade—her pride was probably the only she had left to her name. Whatever that name might be.

He pulled them into a gas station, and Sarah got out of the car to stretch as he filled the truck. He kept his eye on her but she didn't make a run for it, didn't lunge for the squeegee and try to clock him. She sat on his hood, staring across the street at the tiny town center.

"Does this place have a drugstore?" she asked.

Russ didn't respond. He topped off the tank and replaced the pump. He came around and opened her door for her, slammed it as she took a seat. He climbed into the driver's side and started the engine.

She touched his arm, and Russ chose to believe that tingling sensation was his skin crawling, not warming.

"Drugstore? Please?"

Giving her a stern look, he weighed trust against stupidity. He turned them back onto Main Street, holding up the hand he had dangling out the window as he passed a regular client.

"Please, Russ. I haven't felt like a human being in three weeks. If you're going to turn me in tomorrow, give me one day to feel like that again."

"Maybe."

"Look, there's one." She aimed her finger up ahead of them. "Let me just get a couple things."

"Fine." Russ made a left into the pharmacy parking lot. "But I'm coming with you."

They parked and he followed her inside, followed her straight to the women's hygiene section. Russ felt his face go red and rethought this plan. He went to the rear of the store, checking to see the back door was locked. Passing by Sarah again, he kept his eyes off the box she was examining.

"I'll be in the truck."

Sarah stepped out of the store five minutes later with a plastic shopping bag swinging from each hand. As she climbed into the cab and slammed the door, Russ's hammering pulse began to slow.

"Thank you. See? I didn't run off or anything. Just needed some things."

He shifted in his seat. "You got enough money?"

She met his eyes. "Yeah. Enough."

"Where'd you get it?"

Her amber eyes narrowed. "I didn't steal it."

Russ started the truck. "I believe you. But don't sound so defensive, after what happened last night."

"It's the last of my savings," she said quietly.

Russ turned a thought around in his head as he steered them out of town and onto the two-lane highway. "I'll pay you,

you know. If you help me with the chores and the horses. *If* I let you stay."

Neither said anything for over a minute, until Sarah finally asked, "Yeah?"

"Sure. Not a lot. I mean, I'd already be feeding you. But something, so you can maybe save up enough to get someplace, when you're ready to. Again, *if.*"

"When I'm ready to? You mean when you decide it's time to kick me out?"

"I mean the next time you decide you're ready to drug my dogs and run off in the middle of the night. Maybe by then you'll have enough cash for bus fare to wherever you're wanting to go, and if I find my truck and my family heirlooms and my ketamine are still where they should be, I won't run after you."

She made a smug little noise, a laugh or sigh, and the warmth in her voice made Russ's collar feel tight.

"Deal," she said.

He looked at her sideways with a raised eyebrow. She raised one back and put out her hand. Russ gave it a brief, awkward shake then wrapped his own back around the wheel, trying to forget how soft her skin was, how burned he still felt about the sex.

He supposed they both knew what his decision was, then— the one he'd already known he was making the second he pulled away from the police station. He wouldn't be taking her back there tomorrow, not ever, unless she had the gall to screw him over again and get caught at it.

The only place he was taking her was *in,* back into his home. Stupid-ass decision, maybe, but he'd accept whatever bad came of it. Couldn't be worse than leaving her in custody, not knowing her full story.

"You know," he said, thinking out loud, "one of my uncles used to have this old saying about how you could tell a stupid man, because he was one who'd get kicked by a donkey, over and over. And how a smart man was the one who'd get kicked once, then learned to not stand behind a fucking donkey."

She huffed out a tiny laugh. "Okay."

"You're the donkey, Sarah."

"Yeah, I figured as much."

Russ waited for a straight stretch of road then turned to stare at her, waiting until she met his eyes. "I'm not a smart man, so I'm asking now—please don't fucking kick me again." He turned back to the road.

"I promise I won't if you never tell me another hokey country wisdom adage ever again."

Russ smiled grimly to himself, kept his attention trained homeward. "Guess I'll keep the ice handy."

Chapter Seven

During the forty-minute drive home, Russ's heart slowed to a manageable pace. Wrong decision or not, keeping Nicole—no, keeping *Sarah*—here felt right. Or if not right, at least he could breathe again. Still, he was careful to take his keys with him as they left the truck.

He trotted up the steps and unlocked the house, glancing at his prisoner's face as he held the door open. Her hives had faded but her nostrils and lips and ears were still flushed pink.

"Thanks." She slipped by him and went to take a seat at his dining room table.

He followed, dumping his keys on the counter then picking them up again, mustering the good sense to keep them in his pocket. "Don't thank me yet. Like I said, I don't know what I'm going to do with you."

"Why'd you change your mind, at the station?"

Russ bit his lip. He didn't want to give her any insight into what was going on in his head, in case she tried to use it to manipulate him. "That's my business."

"You made it sound like you might let me stay and earn my keep."

"Maybe."

Russ turned as she blew out a deep, heavy sigh. "I'll do whatever you ask me. I promise."

An ache throbbed in his chest, sadness or dread. It was damn tough to see her this way, broken and obedient, when he'd felt so lit up by her feistiness when she'd still been Nicole to him. He wanted some taste of that back, some proof she hadn't faked it all to soften him up, open his home and his heart. "Well, you can start by making breakfast," he said, sitting wearily in the chair beside hers. Their knees were nearly touching, her jeans dark, his faded, both dusty.

She stood, setting her fingers lightly on his shoulder and making him flinch. She took her hand back. "Sorry." She pushed out another almighty sigh, seeming to ground herself in some way. "How many eggs do you want?"

"Three."

"Bacon?"

"Please." The thinnest stream of calm trickled through his body, his muscles releasing some of their tension. He stared out back windows, remembering his duties. "I have to feed the animals."

"Okay. I'll be right here."

"Good." He grabbed his rifle as he stood, and her eyes followed the action. Guilt fisted his guts. "It's so you won't shoot me. Not because I'm planning on shooting you, if you run."

She nodded and swallowed, looking as uncomfortable as Russ felt.

"I'll be right out back."

Another nod and Russ went out the rear door, taking in the cool air in deep, greedy gulps, so deep he felt his mind swim. He stared at the rifle in his hand, felt the keys in his pocket and wondered how he'd become this man so quickly. Lover one night, jailer the next. Tomorrow, maybe sucker again. He released a breath and chased it with a curse.

He checked the dogs first, finding them milling around the backyard, groggy but happy, hungry as always. No harm, no foul...no chance he'd be forgetting it anytime soon, though. Pathetic as it was, those dogs were his closest friends. He fed them and tended to the horses and stood still, staring at the far-off mountains for a long time. A knock on the window made him jump. He looked up to find Sarah on the other side of the glass, holding up a spatula.

He nodded then gave his property a final looking-over. Part of him dreaded going back inside. She was the one under house arrest, but Russ could feel his breath turning short, claustrophobic at the thought of sharing such a small space with her...with the body of the false woman he'd just about fallen in love with, suddenly inhabited by the real one who'd betrayed him. He checked his phone, praying for a job to rescue him. Nothing. He tucked it away and headed for the back steps.

Sarah finished washing the dishes and stole a glance behind her at where Russ was flipping through the paper. Everything was as it had been the day before, only utterly different. They hadn't shared a single word as they ate, each lost in private thoughts. As she turned off the tap and dried her hands, she tried to muster the breath necessary to speak, to ask Russ what she should be doing—

"That was good," he said, eyes still on the paper. "Thanks."

"You're welcome." Relief bloomed in her heart for a second, swiftly replaced by fresh guilt. "What else can I do for you?"

Russ's chest swelled with a deep inhalation. He finally looked up, weariness dripping from every handsome feature on his face. "How'd you sleep last night?"

She wondered if he meant that accusingly, as in how had she found the gall to get any rest after what she'd done? But his expression told her it was merely a question. "Pretty horribly. Sort of wish you'd shot those tranquilizers at me after all."

Russ's smile was tight and humorless. "I figured. I got a ton of paperwork to take care of. You go ahead and take a nap, if you feel like it." He nodded to the couch and its pile of blankets, and Sarah had to admit, it looked like heaven after the drama and anxiety and mistakes of the previous night.

"I'd like that."

Russ shrugged. "Have at it. I'll wake you this afternoon when it's time for chores."

She swallowed an urge to ask how he felt toward her and if he was going to let her stay. And if he did, how long they'd be this way, her the criminal and Russ the parole officer. She regretted what she'd done back in Buffalo, and until this morning she thought she'd never regret anything that badly for the rest of her life. But this, seeing the kindest man she'd ever met so clearly disappointed and untrusting... This hurt worse. Right now she'd give anything to fix what she'd wrecked, or maybe to have never crossed paths with Russ Gray in the first place. He deserved her like he deserved a kick in the teeth, the way she deserved a second chance—not at all.

Sarah watched him clearing the dining room table as she settled into the blankets, and she saw the biggest regret of her life standing there by the window. She had another urge to run, run far and fast until her lungs burst, if only to stand a chance of forgetting what they'd had for two glorious nights, the thing she'd wrecked, just like she'd known she would.

By ten that evening, Russ's anger had faded from an open wound to a bruise. He and Sarah had spoken plenty in the last few hours, instructions politely requested and tendered as she helped with the chores. He'd switched the radio on during dinner and let the news fill the hole where flirtation and chitchat had been this time yesterday. He had no clue how to feel toward this woman. She was his lover, formerly a friend,

115

now a stranger. Russ punched the pillows on his bed, listening to the sound of water flowing on the other side of the wall in the bathroom.

He stripped to his boxers and pulled on a clean T-shirt, staring at the bed. Keeping her in here was wrong. Not morally wrong; he had a right to be distrustful. But it felt weird, given the sexual tension they'd shared, to say nothing of what had gone on in this bed between them. Russ sank onto the edge of the mattress and rubbed his face.

"Knock knock."

He looked up to find Sarah in the threshold, expression soft and timid.

"You want something to sleep in?"

She looked to her jeans. "If you're offering, sure."

He got up and rummaged in his dresser, tossed her a shirt and shorts. He busied himself setting his alarm clock while she changed. When the time came for them both to get into bed, Russ felt the itchiness dogging his conscience come to a head.

He stared at the bed and dragged a hand through his hair. "You um... You shouldn't have to sleep with me."

"It's okay, Russ. I want you to trust me. It's not the most terrible price in the world to pay."

He met her eyes and found good-natured sadness there. "Makes me feel like a creep. Like I'm..." He trailed off.

"You're not a creep. *I'm* the creep."

Russ sighed, done with this talk, weary of her apologies and his own hurt. He strode to the lights and switched them off, waiting for her to get comfortable under the covers before he joined her. He slid between the comforter and the top sheet, a diplomatic layer between their bodies in case one of them rolled over in the night. His bed was big and he gave her plenty of space, an unspoken correction of the previous night's physical restraint. Arms folded atop the covers, Russ stared at the faint slice of deep blue moonlight striping his ceiling and prayed for sleep to come quickly. After a minute the sheets rustled as Sarah rolled over to face him.

"Russ?"

He swallowed, her voice seeming so close in the darkness, so intimate and familiar. "Yeah?"

"Tomorrow... Do you think you're going to turn me in? I'm sorry, it's unfair to ask. But it's torture, not knowing."

He took a deep breath, then another. "No. I'm not going to turn you in."

A pause, more rustling. "No?"

"No. I couldn't do it when I was pissed to high heaven, and I know I won't be able to now I've calmed down. That might make me the world's biggest sucker, but..."

"I won't run."

"Even if you do, just tell me first. I'll give you a little money, a lift to a bus station maybe." Russ's chest loosened from hearing himself articulate these things, from committing to a decision, even if it might prove a foolish one.

He heard Sarah's head shift on the pillow and when she spoke her mouth sounded impossibly near. "That'd make you some kind of accomplice."

"It'd make me some kind of idiot too. But when I see the back of you, I want to think maybe you're going to be okay. Not still peppered with holes, hitching rides."

"Okay."

"You want me to draw you an insulting analogy?" Russ asked, smirking into the dark.

"Not if it means I get called a donkey again."

"I was thinking a dog," he said. "Anyhow, I've been bitten by lots of dogs since I became a vet, a couple coyotes, a wolf once..."

117

"Uh-huh."

"All of them scared or sick or abused by somebody. And I still patched them up and sent them on their way. That's what I'm doing for you."

"You make those mean dogs sleep in your bed with you?"

Russ's weak smile faded to nothing. "No, I don't. Sorry."

"I'm just teasing you. Like I've got any leverage to complain."

"No, you're right." He pushed himself up and peeled the covers back. "You're free to sleep where you want. You're not my prisoner."

She didn't move or speak.

"Sarah?"

"No...thank you for that, but it's fine. I'm already sort of comfy in here."

It was Russ's turn to hesitate. Now that he'd abandoned his earlier reasoning, forcing her to share his bed seemed ludicrous. "Fine. You stay here then." He rolled to the edge of the mattress, getting to his feet and grabbing his pillow.

"Russ."

"Yeah?"

Again a pause. "I feel like a jerk, driving you out of your own bed. I'll take the couch."

"I don't care. You're comfortable."

"Yeah, but—"

"Don't worry about it. I'll see you in the morning."

"Okay. Good night."

He closed the door behind him, stumbling in the darkness to the cold leather couch to assemble the pile of blankets into an imitation of order. He got settled and stared at the dark blue squares of the windowpanes to his side, letting himself feel the antsy energy warming his body and admitting it was sexual.

He'd made a decision to let her back into his home—his bed, even—expose his valuables to her, his hospitality, not to mention his trust, as tempered with skepticism as it was. Even his dignity, he was laying that on the line, hoping she wouldn't run off into the darkness with it if she stabbed him in the back again. Still, his heart and his traitorous body—his hope—those he'd be keeping locked away, heck, shackled to his ankle where he'd never lose track of them. If she managed to hack his leg off in the dead of night and take those too...well the fuck with it then.

A strange series of sounds woke Russ early the next day— the muffled bleeps of his alarm, a female yelp, a faint crash and the barks of the dogs outside. He registered where he was and why, then flung the covers away and jogged to his room. He found Nicole—no, Sarah—bent over his nightstand, trying to cancel his alarm.

"What was that crash?" he asked, taking the clock from her and clicking it off.

"That was me knocking your lamp over. But don't worry, it didn't break."

"Well, morning." Russ finally looked her in the eye, seeing his own awkward hesitance reflected right back at him.

"Morning. Heck of a siren you've got there."

"Sorry, it's only got one setting. I usually wake up before it goes off." He'd conditioned himself to do that years ago. Beth had always hated that alarm, always socked him on the shoulder when it went off and burrowed deeper in the covers. Russ's internal clock had long ago adjusted to avoid her wrath.

"Feel free to sleep in, if you're still tired," Russ said.

"Nah, that's okay."

They went about dressing, tugging their jeans on with a synchrony that felt satirical. Russ buttoned his shirt and watched from the corner of his eye as she changed her own, not sure what he was looking to find...an old glimmer of attraction, maybe. Maybe nothing at all.

"You like oatmeal?" he asked, making his tone friendly and neutral.

"Whatever's easy. I can make it, if you want."

"It's no trouble." Russ's throat felt tight from the effort it took to keep up this diplomatic charade. He fled to the kitchen to start breakfast. When he heard Sarah close herself in the bathroom, he went to the stereo and turned the radio on again, so stupidly afraid of a conversation when she reappeared.

In ten minutes she came out and seemed to take the hint. She went to her now-usual seat at the dining room table and slid yesterday's paper over, saying nothing. Russ stared into the pot of bubbling oats, inventing a hundred tasks to get them through the day, keep them busy. He didn't think he could stand to hear her apologize to him again. Every sad "I'm sorry" was a pin jabbed in his skin, a stinging reminder of how wrecked everything had become.

When the oatmeal was done, Russ doled it into bowls and set a box of brown sugar on the table between them.

She accepted her cereal with another weak smile, the faintest glimmer of those grins that had set Russ's heart pounding before the betrayal.

"Thanks."

He nodded, sliding the farming section out from the pile of papers and staring at the words all through the meal. She stood first, taking their bowls to the sink. Russ shivered from the familiarity of this routine, from how easy she was to get used to. As funny as it made him feel, he got up and went to the counter, taking the dishes as she rinsed them and blotting them dry with the towel. Somewhere deep and selfish in his body, he wanted to feel that spark between them again, not this heavy weight that had dropped in to take its place.

Sarah handed him the final dish. "Mind if I hole up in the bathroom this morning?"

Russ shrugged agreeably, then went to work making a pot of coffee. God knew he needed it. He'd slept like shit and had more of the literal same to shovel that morning when he mucked the stalls. Sarah took her plastic drugstore bags from the counter and shut herself in the bathroom.

A little while later, camped out on a couch with a steaming mug and clear view of the bathroom window, Russ looked up from the newspaper. He flared his nostrils and frowned in the direction of the closed door, all his suspicion rushing back in to replace the melancholy. He set the paper aside and crossed the den, knocking.

"What's that smell?"

Her muffled reply came through the door. "Hair dye."

"Oh." He didn't know what he'd been expecting—plastic explosives, homemade arsenic, moonshine. A pang twisted in his chest, sadness for this woman whose only privacy was to be found in a stranger's bathroom, reduced to changing who she was to stay free. Or *sort of* free. He made a stab at levity. "What's the hot color for fugitives this season?"

There was a pause, then a faint laugh. Russ could picture her smile and how she must be shaking her head at him. "It's called..."

She opened the door, a pile of slick curls plastered atop her head, eyebrows painted with the dark goo, smears on her temples and ears. She had one of Russ's ratty old towels wrapped around her trunk. His eyes watered from the chemical smell.

She read the top of the box. "Chocolate Truffle," she concluded, smiling at him, those wide lips banishing the fumes for a second as Russ got lost staring at the base of her throat.

"Doesn't smell too delicious," he said, eyes still glued to her collarbone.

Sarah closed the door on him.

"Turn the fan on before you asphyxiate," Russ said.

An hour later she emerged looking different. Not just the dark, damp locks brushing her shoulders—she'd cut off at least four inches—but something about her face too, details Russ was too hopelessly male to pinpoint. He'd always gotten himself in trouble with his wife over things like that, never noticing when she'd gone to trouble with her hair or makeup, earning himself some major eye-rolling.

"Your face looks real nice," Russ said.

Sarah laughed. "Thanks?"

"You know." He waggled a hand in front of his own face. "Your makeup or whatever."

Sarah crossed her arms over her chest, plastic bag swinging from her wrist, and gave him an eye roll that put Beth's to shame. "You're supposed to pretend a woman always looks naturally made-up."

"Oh." Russ blinked at this latest damned-if-you-do, damned-if-you-don't female snare and stepped aside to let Sarah wander past him to sit on the couch.

"Well, you look real nice."

"Thank you." She was wearing her tank top thing and Russ's old boxers, the fly safety-pinned closed. Her bare legs looked smooth, almost shiny. She stretched them out and wiggled her toes. "I feel like a human being again, anyhow. Amazing what deodorant and conditioner and some lotion can do." She opened the shopping bag and drew out a magazine, the glossy kind with a dazzling woman on the cover.

Russ pointed to it. "You've got a handful of dollars left to your name and you spent it on that?"

She lowered the pages, giving him a withering look as she sat up straighter.

"Fine," he said. "I won't argue with that face. I'm just saying, if you'd sold my great-grandfather's watch and spent the spoils on *that*, I'd be mighty pissed."

Her smug expression wilted, replaced by sadness. "Sorry. I guess that does make me look pretty shallow."

Russ returned her frown then walked over and flopped down beside her, watching the pages flip in her lap. "I don't think you're shallow. I just don't follow your priorities."

"Well, imagine if you were exiled in New York City or somewhere for, I don't know, a horse vet convention or something. A whole week stuck in meeting rooms, no fresh air, and even when you're outside it's crammed with strangers and buildings and honking cars."

"Okay."

"How much would you pay just to like, get over to Central Park and smell the stupid horses for a few minutes?"

He considered it, not sure where this ham-fisted analogy was headed. "I couldn't say. Maybe a lot."

"Well," she said, flipping through ads and spreads, an indistinguishable blur of makeup and jewelry and shoes. "This for me...it only cost four bucks, and I get to pretend for an hour or so that I'm still back home, still imagining what I might want to save up and buy for myself."

She set the magazine down and stared Russ square in the face. He looked to her knee, eye contact too much, too likely to just confuse whatever he was feeling. Feeling. He'd started doing too much of that since Sarah had shown up. Or Nicole. Whoever.

"I know you probably don't think I deserve frivolity," she said, "but if I could, I'd go back in time three weeks and I wouldn't be here now, wrecking your life. Or mine. I'd be home on a day off, flipping through a magazine." She shook it at him, subscription cards falling onto their legs. "And maybe having a glass of wine, thinking about what I might wear out to a party or a bar, fantasizing about some nice, handsome guy I might magically meet." She looked down, lips pursed, and Russ suspected she was close to crying. "I'm not supposed to be here, you know, stealing some other nice, handsome guy's heirlooms. I'm supposed to be home, safe and bored. Worried about catching the bus, not about prison or getting knifed by the wrong choice of driver to bum a ride from. So lay off, Russ. Let me read my stupid magazine." She sniffed irritably, ignoring the fat tear slipping down her cheek.

The ugliest, meanest part of Russ searched her face, wondering if this might all be some new con, a ploy for his trust. He didn't want to be that man—suspicious, expecting the worst. But he wasn't aiming to be her fool again, either. In the end he just clapped her on the shoulder and stood, leaving her to her handbags and perfume samples, to her sadness, real or manufactured.

Chapter Eight

Sarah perused her magazine for an hour while Russ was out doing whatever it was he did. She listened through the open kitchen window to the various sounds of his productivity—automotive noises and hammering ones, distant hinges creaking and the odd grunt. She didn't know what it meant that he'd left her alone. *Trust* was too much to hope for, as even she wasn't sure if she'd try to run again.

It sucked to commodify Russ, to see him as an opportunity. Still, that's what he was, in essence—a chance at redemption, should he choose to let her stay. A ticket to prison if he changed his mind and decided that was best. The only power she had now lay in her two feet and how far and fast they could carry her, but three weeks of running had left her exhausted. She wanted to stay with Russ and earn what he'd offered, some money and a safe place to sleep for as long as he'd allow. She said a little prayer to a God she'd never believed in that he'd keep his promise from last night and give her this second chance she didn't particularly deserve.

Out of habit, she dog-eared the magazine's best pages, the things she'd try to copy or find cheapie versions of, should she ever find her herself with extra cash and within a hundred miles of a shopping center. Gift ideas for friends she'd probably never see again. Stupid articles about men to cut out and paste up in the break room to annoy her male coworkers, if only she still had something as normal as a job. These things had always seemed silly, but now it was too much. She'd lost the luxury of wasteful daydreaming. She might never again be in a position to fantasize about a purse or a pair of sunglasses she could buy if the tip gods smiled upon her some Saturday evening. With an annoyed sigh, she tossed the magazine aside and rubbed her temples to banish a headache.

She dropped her hands and gasped, surprised to find Russ standing before her.

"Sorry. Wasn't trying to sneak up on you." He tucked his hands in his pockets.

"That's fine. It's your house." She studied the black grease smear on his arm.

"You um…you want to go for a ride?"

She frowned, transported mentally to the police station parking lot again. "Where to?"

He shrugged and nodded toward the back of the house. "Just around."

"Oh, you mean on a horse?"

"Yeah. One of those things you groomed the other day. The huge, furry, smelly things that crap everywhere?"

She considered it. "Do I get a saddle?"

"Sure."

"I guess I could try that."

"Cool." He glanced at her feet. "My sister's got a pair of boots she keeps here that'll probably fit you. We can go and mess up your pretty new hairdo."

Sarah tugged on her filthy sneakers. Following Russ out back, she waited as he laced his shoes in the laundry room. He rummaged for a couple of minutes and found her a pair of riding boots, tight but workable.

"Where are we riding to?"

"Just around the property."

Property, she thought. *Territory.* She remembered that possessive quality she'd felt in his touch before she'd gone and screwed all that up for them both.

Russ fitted Lizzie with a blanket and saddle and bridle. He led her out into the pen, looking expectantly to Sarah.

She wrung her hands. "I'm not sure how to do this."

"Get your left foot in the stirrup, and hold on to her mane—don't yank it—and swing your right leg up and over." He held Lizzie's bridle, pale eyes squinting against the sunshine.

Sarah got her foot in the stirrup, hand on the horse's knobby neck. "They should make stairs for this."

"Just do it. Don't think."

Right. That philosophy had gotten her in enough trouble to last a lifetime. But she pushed off the ground and with a little shimmying, lo and behold, there she was, perched on a horse.

Russ handed her the reins. "Just sit tight. Don't pull on those."

She watched him lead Mitch out into the dusty ring, walking him to the far stretch of fence, where Russ lifted a catch and pulled the gate open. He did his little cowboy trick, flinging himself on Mitch's back. He turned and made a clicking noise, and Lizzie started walking, startling the bejesus out of Sarah.

"What do I do?" she asked, one hand in a death grip on the knob at the front of her saddle, the other clutching the reins.

"Nothing," he said over his shoulder. "Just don't panic and focus on your balance. She's driving so sit back and relax."

"Uh-huh."

"Lizzie's not the brightest horse I ever met, but nothing spooks her. You'll be fine as long as you don't faint and fall off."

"And if I do?"

"If you can find your rhythm, just let your body move with hers."

It took a good ten minutes, but Sarah did relax. She tried to imitate how Russ rode, with that lilt in his hips to offset the movement of the horse. He led them along a well-worn dirt trail through his property's overgrown grass, taking them into the shade along the edge of the woods. The dogs followed, trotting behind them like an entourage.

"How we doing?" Russ asked, craning to catch her eye.

"Not bad. I'm still upright."

He slowed, clicked at Lizzie until she came forward to walk side by side with Mitch.

"You look about right. Bit hunchy." He slouched forward, shoulders bunched around his ears.

Sarah sat up straighter, mustering dignity.

"Better."

"Do you know how good you have it?" she asked, surprising even herself with the question.

"How good I have it?"

"That it's like a Monday afternoon—"

"Tuesday."

"A Tuesday afternoon, and you're like, on a horse, patrolling your vast, waving acres."

"Yeah, and an hour ago I was shoveling manure, and tomorrow I'll probably have my arm jammed halfway up a cow's backside."

She smirked. "Well it all seems very luxurious to me. Nobody's got a yard where I'm from, let alone all this." She nodded in the direction of his home.

"They probably don't have to drive an hour to the store either, or spend years waiting for an eligible member of the opposite sex to stroll into the same zip code."

She caught and held his eyes, leaned over and let his greener grass whap her hand demonstrably. Russ just smiled his private smile, eyes on the land.

A half-mile onward Sarah gathered enough balls to clear her throat and say, "You know, I'm really sorry about what happened."

Russ flinched, if she wasn't mistaken. "I know you are. And I believe you. You don't have to keep apologizing."

"My name really is Sarah," she said. "Sarah Novak."

Russ turned to her. "Middle name?"

"Jean."

"Right, Sarah Jean Novak."

"I lived in Buffalo. Like my whole life. If you Google me, you might find out there's a warrant for my arrest."

His eyebrows rose but he didn't reply.

"I'm not actually sure," she said.

"Okay."

"But I killed somebody."

Russ nodded grimly, as though he'd already prepared himself for a worst-case scenario. "Who?"

"This guy... He was my friend's boyfriend, or her dealer or something. I only kind of knew him from around the neighborhood. And actually she wasn't even really my friend anymore. She called me up the night it happened, after we hadn't talked in a couple months. And we used to be really close, like in high school and for a few years after. Before she got all involved with him and these other sketchy assholes." She looked to Russ, wondering if this information was what he deserved or merely another burden he was willing to take on.

"Go on."

"Do you actually want to hear all this?"

He nodded. "Yeah. I think you owe me some insight."

"Okay. Anyhow, this former friend called me, freaking out. I'm sure she was drunk or high or something. I was a little drunk too, out at a bar, watching a baseball game with one of my coworkers. She was only a few blocks away, and I ran over there, to her boyfriend's place. You could hear them yelling from the street, like four stories down. One of them buzzed me in and I ran up there and she was in her underwear, all strung out, with this huge red bruise on her throat. And I don't know...I lost it. I started screaming, saying I was going to call the cops, then the boyfriend freaked out, and he started yelling at *her* for calling *me*, started threatening us both. He hit her, and I just...I saw red. He had one of those old blenders on his counter, the heavy glass kind, and I grabbed it by the handle and I..." She could almost hear the dull clunk it'd made, just about feel the jarring echo of the impact in her wrist. "I hit him. In the head. Hard. And there was blood just...everywhere." Her heart pounded, adrenaline from that night coursing fresh in her veins.

Russ stared at her for a minute. "Isn't that self-defense, though? Maybe?"

"My friend told me she was going to call the police on me," Sarah said. "She told me I murdered him and she started screaming about the death penalty or something crazy, and I bolted, afraid the neighbors were already dialing 9-1-1."

"And you just ran?"

"I had about five hundred dollars in my checking account, and I hit a few ATMs, withdrew the limit until I drained it. I rode around on the city buses with no plan, no clue what to do, ended up crashing at an ex's place for the night. And the next day I found a bus line that didn't ask for ID and I just...left. I went to Des Moines, then Denver, then I ran low on cash so I started hitching in Wyoming."

"You can't go back and tell the police what happened?"

"She won't corroborate my story, and the bruise she had, it must be gone by now, so I can't prove he hurt her. Plus I don't have a real stellar record. Shoplifting and some fights when I was younger. My legal karma's pretty bleak. And I mean, I ran. That can't look good."

"And you won't face the time you might be due?"

She took a deep breath, staring down at her hands on the front of the saddle. "I know, it sounds so cowardly. But it could be a *lot* of time. And this is probably going to sound *really* ridiculous...I'm claustrophobic. I can't tell you how much of a non-option prison is to me. I'd seriously rather be on the run. I'd rather live in fear than in a cage."

"I can't fault anyone for trying to preserve their freedom." Russ stared up into the trees to their right, as if he was thinking exactly what she was, how heavenly all this space was—how necessary.

"But what about your family?" he asked, meeting her eyes. "Aren't there people back there missing you? Worried about you?"

"No, not really. I don't have any family. A few friends, but no one so close to me that I'd risk trying to reach them, you know?"

"I don't, but I'm trying to understand... Can I ask where your parents are?"

"My mom died two years ago. And I never knew my dad."

"No siblings?"

"None I know about."

"Oh."

He sounded sad, so sad she wanted to reach across and hug him, remind him she didn't deserve his sympathy, as comforting as it felt.

"What did you do for work, before you took off?" he asked.

"Tended bar. I never went to college...though I sort of still wanted to, up until last month. But I was always lousy at school. I'm dyslexic and I was way behind everybody by the time anybody figured it out. By then I hated everything about school. Everything but art classes and track." She finger-combed her loose hair, twisting it into a knot and snapping an elastic around it. "God, you must think I'm such a loser, telling you all this. That I'm twenty-eight next month, and I've got no career and a criminal record and probably a murder warrant—"

"I don't think that."

"No?"

"No." He gazed out across the grass in the waning afternoon sun, hat casting a shadow over half his face. "Trust me, I've got no clue who you are yet, but I don't think you're a loser. Outlaw, maybe." He straightened up, smiling at her. "Very exciting."

"I'll bet."

"Most exciting thing that's happened around here in ages."

"Do you believe me, about how things happened?"

Russ didn't reply right away and she couldn't blame him. "I honestly don't know. But I figure I have two choices. I choose to believe you, then I'm either a nice, forgiving person or a sucker twice-over. If I choose to assume you're lying, then I'm either smart or an asshole. Think I'd probably rather be a sucker than an asshole, so I guess I'm choosing to believe you."

It didn't feel like a victory, Russ's limp offer of trust. It smacked of pity and duress. Sarah sighed to herself as she stared down at Lizzie's steady, lumpy shoulder muscles working. "This isn't how I imagined my life would end up. For all the shit I've gotten myself into, I never thought I'd find myself doing this. Running."

"I'm sure nobody ever does."

She took a deep breath. "You know what happened between us..."

"Yeah?"

"Physically, I mean. I just want to say again, that wasn't anything aside from what it seemed like. I wasn't trying to get into your good graces or anything. That was all real for me. It actually..." She laughed. "It actually sucked, hearing you call me Nicole. You don't know how bad I wanted to set you straight about my name."

Russ licked his lips, shy or nervous.

"But for all the other ways I've lied and screwed you over, that wasn't one of them. Not to me, anyhow."

"Thanks... I have to wonder, why did you run?" he asked. "From me, I mean. Why was that an option, when telling me the truth, asking to stay for a while, wasn't?"

She frowned, sad about her answer. "I didn't know what you'd say or do. I didn't know how angry you'd be about me turning up here as like, a fugitive, making you an accessory, maybe. However that works. Or how you'd feel when you realized I'd lied to you. You seem like a real good guy, Russ—like the kind of good they don't make on the east side of Buffalo. Real straight-and-narrow, guns and justice. I thought there was a decent chance you'd turn me in. And I didn't want you to know what a lousy person I am, frankly. Or at least I didn't want to have to see your face when you found out. Ideally I just wanted to disappear, leave you thinking I was better than I really am, maybe even missing me. But right now I have to put money and survival above saving face."

Russ nodded and gave Mitch a few pats on the neck. "That's real sad."

"Sad like, pathetic, or sad like..."

"Like I feel sad for you. No pity, no judging. It's just real sad. Sad like when a friend loses a parent or a child. Sad like your life's changed and nobody can change it back. Like grief."

Something about that word was too much. Sarah prayed Russ would keep his eyes on the path when the tears started, and she kept her own eyes on Lizzie's mane so she wouldn't have to know if her crying had a witness. Grief was exactly it. Her old life was dead, and she'd woken up here, in a beautiful place she envied but didn't belong in, nothing familiar to be found in all these acres of somebody else's freedom.

They rode in silence for a long time, Russ leading them single file through a path in the woods. The tears cleaned Sarah out and left her calmer. She watched her host's back, feeling comfortable for once, tucked safely behind him, relegated to Lizzie's burden, allowed to follow and ride, to turn off her own momentum and simply be carried.

"Russ?"

"Yeah."

"You know that room past your bedroom?"

He glanced over his shoulder at her. "Uh-huh."

"What's in there? Is it another bedroom?"

"Supposed to be. You think I'd stick you on the couch if it was habitable?" He smiled, something not quite comfortable about the gesture, then faced forward.

"Can I ask what's in there? Is it your wife's things or...?"

"Oh, I see what you're getting at. And yes. And no. Not the way you mean."

"You don't have any pictures of her out or anything."

He slowed Mitch and let Lizzie catch up so he and Sarah were side by side again. "No, I don't, you're right. They're in albums. Those memories are complicated... I like to think about that stuff on purpose, I guess. Sit down and do it properly, not glance at a frame and suddenly get all thrown into it."

"You've got plenty of pictures up of your great-grandfather."

"Yeah, but that's different. He died when he was a hundred and three. That's fair. What happened to my wife was unfair, and thinking about it makes me real angry sometimes."

"Oh."

"And that room's full of all kinds of stuff. Books and projects I've half-finished, boring things. And some other things, the type of things you're thinking about. Her wedding dress is in there. And, um, some baby furniture." He met her eyes and smiled tightly.

Sarah went numb. "Oh. Was she...?"

"No, she wasn't, but we were headed in that direction. Getting excited about it, starting to turn that room into a nursery and all that. I'm a practical man, but I haven't quite had it in me to disassemble the crib and haul it into town to the thrift shop. At first you know, it was too hard. Now it's just that I've gotten used to that room being a mess."

"Understandable."

"And part of it's because I *am* practical. I'd like a family someday, and I thought hell, I might need a crib again, who knows? Not that things are looking too likely seven years on. Lately I've been thinking I need to clear that room out...it's the place where projects go to die. Some black hole for good intentions."

"Maybe my old life is buried in there someplace."

Russ laughed, out of politeness she guessed.

"If you want, I'll clean it out for you," Sarah said. "As one of my chores."

Russ nodded in time with Mitch's steps, looking thoughtful. "That's not a bad idea."

"What would you do if you did have a free room?"

"Well it used to be the guest room, where our parents or my sisters would sleep when they came to visit. But I kind of stopped volunteering to host family holidays after my wife died. Like the venue was too depressing and might bring everybody down."

"I used to host this thing I called Homeless Thanksgiving," Sarah offered. "I'd invite all my friends who were like me, not close with their families, and the ones who couldn't travel home for whatever reason. I'd cram twenty people into my one-bedroom apartment, and we'd eat supermarket rotisserie chicken and macaroni and cheese and drink wine and play board games."

Russ stared at her face for a few beats. "You sound like you miss that."

She smiled down at her hands. "I will, I bet. When November rolls around. But people are adaptable. Who knows where I'll be this year. Maybe Mexico, so there won't even be a Thanksgiving to worry about."

Russ studied her for a moment.

"What?"

He looked ahead again as Mitch brought them back out into the fields. "If you don't screw me over before you leave...if you ever find yourself back around here at Christmastime or whenever, you feel free to come by. I'll drive you to Idaho and my mother will stuff you silly."

She chewed her lip to stifle a grin.

"Actually," Russ went on, "I could pay you to pretend to be my girlfriend so she'll stop asking about my love life and the dwindling male branches of the Gray family tree."

"Right, that'd go well. 'Hi, Mom, this is Sarah. What does she do? Oh, you know, she's a fugitive. Murdered this guy in Buffalo with a blender? Yeah, long story. So when's dinner?'"

They sank into silence, comfortable again by some miracle of the awkward conversational topic. The horses aimed them home as the sun sank low. Russ hopped off to open the gate, and Lizzie and Mitch headed into the pen. He offered a hand, and Sarah managed to dismount with a modicum of dignity.

She helped him feed the horses and watched him putter in the lengthening shadows. It hurt. He was the kindest, best-looking man she'd ever had a chance with, just another good thing she'd lost now.

He finished his nightly checks and met her by the back door to ditch their boots. "How're your legs?"

She shifted from one foot to the other. "Hips are a bit sore, but it feels good. Like I accomplished something."

He nodded.

"Thank you, for taking me out. You're being really nice, and I'm the last person who deserves it."

Russ shrugged. "Won't make me feel any better to be a jerk to you." He held the door open.

"Thanks... Do you hate me?"

Russ's answer came quick and without bitterness. "I hate what you did to me. But I like *you*. I like the woman I'm choosing to believe you are." He shut the door behind them.

"The one who killed someone?"

He shoved his hands in his front pockets and met her eyes. "I don't even know how to begin to think about that yet. But I like certain things about you. I think you talk a lot of sense, even if half the time I don't understand or agree with you." He pinched two fingers together, nearly touching. "I'm actually about this close to thinking I sort of admire you for having the balls to drug my dogs and rob me in the dead of night. I want to wring your neck, but I also think you might be sort of special."

She made a skeptical face.

"Anyway..." Russ trailed off, scanning the room. "Why don't you take it easy until dinner? I have to return a couple phone calls and do some more paperwork. I'll make something in a bit."

Her heart sank. "You sure there's nothing else I can do to help?"

"Not really."

She sighed, took a chance and made a joke. "You have a harmonica I could play? Maybe a tin can to rattle against the bars when I get hungry?"

Russ's face flipped through a range of emotions before settling on a sad smile. "I really don't have any easy chores to give you, but if you're bored, how about a puzzle or something?"

She laughed. "Yeah, sure."

Russ headed to the door past his bedroom, the so-called black hole for good intentions. Sarah followed as he went inside, scouting around for tragic souvenirs but not finding any obvious ones. Aside from the crib. That was sitting by the far wall under a curtained window, cardboard boxes stacked neatly inside it.

Russ walked to a bookshelf and waved his hand at a selection of board games and jigsaw puzzles. "Have at it." Seeming cagey about being in the room, he left her alone.

Sarah slid out a thousand-piece puzzle of what she thought was a Montana landscape, only to discover it was Idaho when she looked at the lid. "Close enough."

She tucked it under her arm, the rattle of the pieces and the promise of this activity comforting. She bet she hadn't done a puzzle in fifteen years, but she anticipated the smell of musty cardboard already, the perfect fragrance to complement Russ's dated interior decorating.

Closing the door softly behind her, Sarah crossed the den and eyed the coffee table, hoping it was big enough. She opened the box and propped the lid against the arm of the couch beside her for reference. Whoever had done this puzzle last had been lazy, and she set to work breaking up the chunks of linked pieces, wanting to do it properly. She gave a small jump as Russ clunked an open beer bottle before her on the table.

"A thousand pieces," he said. "That'll keep you busy."

"That's what I need."

He nodded. "My grandpa said it was cheating to look at the box. He used to give me and my sisters puzzles for Christmas, but he'd dump all the pieces in a paper bag and throw the packaging away."

Sarah laughed. "God, that's hardcore." For a second she met Russ's eyes, caught there as they shared a smile, caught for the briefest moment in how they'd been two days ago. She turned her attention to the box, sifting for edge pieces.

Russ lingered, as though poised to say something. Instead he wandered back to the dining room table, to whatever papers he was tending to. Sarah glanced at him. After a minute she stood to walk to the record player.

"Tell me when you need it quiet for your phone calls," she said, flipping through his albums. She found that one from her first evening here, Hank Williams with his cartoon body. She set it gently on the turntable and lowered the needle, let everything *Russ* about the music and the room and the land outside the windows envelope her.

He looked up from his work and offered a quick smile, a second's polite effort that warmed her through like a bonfire.

He wasn't her warden anymore, and this house wasn't her prison. Still, it wasn't *hers,* and might not even be the home of a friend. She settled back on the couch and let the puzzle distract her from the body seated across the room, the man she still wanted—wanted worse than she wanted her old life back, maybe. At some point she'd become a lousy person, one who stole from kind strangers and lied about who she really was, ran away from her mistakes. She picked up the box lid and slid it beneath the couch. For everything she'd done badly, she'd do this right. Piece by blind piece, she'd pretend she could fix what she'd so massively screwed up with Russ.

Chapter Nine

By five thirty that evening a heavy rain was falling. By six o'clock Russ had a chicken in the oven, by six fifteen a fire in the hearth. Rain, dinner, fire... Russ wondered if his prisoner-cum-guest was noticing how romantic all these details felt. A knot formed in his chest, good old classic heartache as he registered it again—he missed her. Nicole. He missed a woman who'd never really existed. Now the loss was magnified, punctuated by Sarah's new hair color and the makeup darkening her eyelashes and fading her freckles. Still, he knew it was her. Same body. Same passion, if she hadn't faked it. Same fingers he'd felt digging into his back, same mouth that'd singed his skin—

Russ cleared his head of such thoughts and dusted the flecks of firewood from his palms on his jeans. He crossed the room to crouch on the opposite side of the coffee table, to see how Sarah was progressing with the puzzle. He kept his eyes on the tabletop for safety, away from her face.

"Not quite as far as I'd expected you get in two hours." He watched her audition one piece of sky against a dozen identically blue ones.

"I took a page out of your grandfather's book," she said, finding a match. "I hid the box."

Russ smiled at that. "Technically, he'd be disappointed you even saw the picture to begin with, but still. You're a better man than I."

He caught her smirk, her attention on her fingers. "I doubt that."

Russ held his tongue but didn't move his eyes away quick enough when she looked up at him.

"I meant what I said before," she murmured, more bashful than flirtatious. "You're the best man I've ever met."

Russ stood before she could make an addendum about being a lousy woman, yet another apology he couldn't stand to listen to. He went to the silent record player to cue up a new album just as thunder rumbled outside. The rain picked up along with the wind, and Russ made out the sound of a whine from the porch. He opened the front door and glared at Kit through the screen.

"What?"

Another whimper.

Russ opened the screen door an inch and waited. The dog gave an almighty shake, flinging the rain from her fur. Russ pushed the door out and let her inside. "Stay."

She sank obediently onto the mat just inside the entryway, head on her paws, brows shifting in that self-pitiful way she'd practically patented.

"Pathetic," Russ muttered, and headed back to the coffee table.

Sarah smirked at him. "Somebody afraid of thunder?"

"Yeah. The dog who picks fights with bears...one little flash of lightning and she turns into a bunny."

Sarah smiled, sliding pieces around on the wood. "Dinner smells good."

"Yeah, smells just about done, actually." He watched her fingers, nails short and tidy now, the scrapes from when she'd first arrived here fading already. As much as Russ missed the illusion that was Nicole, he didn't miss that woman's wounds—not the ones on the surface, anyhow. And as much as Russ resented some facets of Sarah, she was real. The circumstances that had brought her here were real, if ugly, but that trumped the mysterious omissions of the woman Russ had fallen so hard for.

Sarah addressed Russ's prolonged scrutiny of her fingers. "You're welcome to help, you know."

"Oh, that's okay. I just spaced out for a minute."

"Long day?"

Russ nodded. "I better check on the roast."

"Yeah."

The chicken was ready, and Russ nearly dropped it, thunder booming just as he was lifting the dish from the oven. He set it on a burner, frazzled. As he slid the mitts off, he listened to the rain, hammering now. "Jesus."

"Yeah," Sarah said. "That was only two Mississippis away."

Kit whimpered but stayed obediently glued to the doormat.

As Russ carved the chicken, the power went out entirely. "Heh." He waited for it to flicker back on, but nothing. He rummaged in the junk drawer for a lighter and lit the two dusty candles on the ledge beside the contentious gold watch. Leaving one in the kitchen, he carried the other to the dining room table. Perfect. This scene would be hard-pressed to turn any more pointedly romantic.

"Just when I thought this puzzle couldn't get any harder," Sarah said.

Russ glanced at her in the low firelight, squinting at the pieces. "Yeah, my grandpa missed a trick. If he really wanted us kids to work, he'd have made us put those together in the dark."

"Or spray painted the pieces black." She seemed to give up on the project, standing and wandering over to take a seat at the dinner table.

Russ went back to carving, mangling the meat in the dim light and serving up a plate for each of them. As he sat across from her, he missed the music, the records' scratched and tinny voices a better excuse to not speak than the din of the rain.

What was he afraid of, anyhow? Of her, really, of them talking, getting friendly again. Of discovering she still resembled the woman he had feelings for and getting himself mixed up in the head, mixed up in a doomed attraction. It was damn hard to tamp all those feelings down after missing them for seven years, though. But the stakes were too high. He could give in if she made a move on him again, tonight or next week or next month, but he'd have to chance waking up to find out it was another ploy. Or worse, he could make a move himself, get rebuffed and discover everything they'd shared had been a lie, as fabricated as her name.

The rain and low rumbles of thunder, the squeak of their knives and forks—the sounds all faded as she spoke, her voice warming the space between them. "So tell me something about yourself, Russ."

"Like what?"

"Oh, anything. Have you traveled much?"

He shook his head. "Farthest I've been is Virginia. And Canada's the only other country I've been to. I don't even have a passport."

"I've barely even been there. Just over the border a couple of times."

"Where, then?" he asked, surprised by how much he suddenly wanted this conversation and its normality.

"Nowhere, practically. Here's the farthest. I've traveled more in the last three weeks than the rest of my life combined, probably. I mean, I've been to New York City a bunch, and Florida, once, when I was little, before my mom...before everything got really rough."

"Before your mom what?"

She frowned at her plate. "She was sort of a mess. But there were two years or so when I was a kid, maybe in first and second grades, when she was clean. That's when we went to Florida."

Russ got up and fetched two more beers, setting them down as distant lightning lit up the horizon. "Can I ask, you know, what she was..."

"God, everything. I don't really want to get into the details. Just some bad stuff."

"Tell me—" Thunder crashed, cutting Russ off. "Tell me about Florida, then."

Sarah paused then broke into a broad smile, staring at her food. "I don't remember much, but I remember a dress I wore. It was yellow. And we went to Disney World, and there was a woman dressed up as a princess or a fairy or something, and she had a yellow dress too, only it was all covered in sequins and shiny stuff. I wanted that dress so bad." She laughed, pushing potatoes around her plate with her fork. "It's weird, but I can still remember it now, like it's right here in front of me."

Russ let his brain make a bad decision and picture Sarah in a dress, instead of the jeans and sneakers and cream-colored shirt she'd arrived in. He realized then he knew next to nothing about her, only her circumstances and a few garments, snatches of shared memory. But he knew other things as well...how she tasted and smelled, how her skin felt against his.

"I remember balloons too," she added. "The really shiny silver Mylar kind, shaped like the Mickey Mouse logo."

145

"Weird, the stuff our kid brains chose to fixate on," Russ said. "I remember smells from before I even have memories to match to them... I blew my mom's mind once, when I smelled some flower or other in the grocery store and said, 'Oh, I remember that flower. And a yellow house and black dog.' I guess it was my aunt's house, where she hadn't lived since I was about a year old."

"Freaky. But I know what you mean. Smell's supposed to be the most deeply engrained sense, or something. I think I read that in one of my stupid magazines."

Lightning flashed again and Russ shifted in his seat. "They're not stupid. If they make you happy, they're not stupid."

"It's okay, I mean they *are* pretty stupid. Have you ever read any of the dating advice in those things?"

He shook his head. "Maybe I should. I could use all the help I can get."

She waved her fork at him dismissively. "Nah. You'd do just fine, if only there were some women around here to woo."

Against his better judgment, Russ glanced at her neck, the dip at base of her throat. He knew exactly how that skin smelled...yet another olfactory memory he'd be stuck carrying to his grave. He corralled his gaze back to his plate, and they passed the rest of the meal quietly, the din of the rain interrupted with the occasional rumble of thunder and Sarah's Mississippi-counting. The storm seemed to be moving off, the rain turning from a pelt to a patter against the back windows. Russ didn't hold out much hope for the power to come back on. They'd probably have to wait for a downed line to be mended the next morning.

Sarah set her napkin on her plate and leaned back in her seat. "That was delicious. Yet another talent you're denying the single women of the world, hiding yourself away in the middle of nowhere."

"I don't know about that." Russ got up and they cleared the table together. He carried the candle from the dining area to the counter, and they tidied the kitchen, stacking the dishes in the sink to tackle once the power came back on. He wanted to blame the waning storm for the buzz he felt in his body...fat chance. A foot separated their hips, and Russ imagined those mad-scientist contraptions from old movies, two metal antennae with waves of crackling electricity strung between them. He wondered if she felt it too, all this hot, antsy energy.

With the kitchen organized and the storm fading, Russ ushered Kit back outside then grabbed both candles and carried them to the coffee table. They cast a sheen across the puzzle pieces, making it nearly impossible to see the picture. Russ sifted through the box, searching for a few missing edge pieces. Sarah returned from a trip to the bathroom and sat beside him, squinting at the project.

"Your grandpa would've approved," she said, angling a piece to make out its colors.

"Probably. He's still alive, actually." Russ swallowed and found the courage to keep talking. "Sharp as he ever was. If you're still here around the holidays and you did end up coming to Idaho, you could meet him."

"If I came along to play the part of your girlfriend and get your mom off your back?"

"Yeah." Russ had to give them credit. It was bold of them to be able to banter this way so soon after their doomed affair had ended. But he liked it. He liked that neither was too sensitive to joke about it, liked that their rapport was there, as strong with Sarah as it had been with Nicole. He might even like that they were flirting, as much as it scared him.

"What would your parents think if you brought home some city girl?" Sarah asked, moving pieces around.

"Oh, they're pretty good with all that stuff. My older sister lives in Seattle, and my younger one spent ten years in San

Francisco before she moved back to Idaho. And I mean compared to my parents, I'm like Daniel Boone, out here. My mom can't stand that I don't have internet access. She's obsessed with all that social-networking nonsense."

Sarah laughed. "Oh God, I'd love to see your profile. Russ Gray, thirty-six. Status, single. Currently listening to Hank Williams, yet again. April tenth, shoved my arm up a cow's ass. July third, got kicked by a mule. Frowny face icon."

Russ took a chance and met her eyes, smirking. "If I knew what any of that meant, I'm sure I'd be insulted."

He got stuck then, staring at her. She seemed trapped too, and all at once the foot between them felt like an inch. *Look away,* Russ commanded himself. Sarah's lips twitched, and Russ felt his own parting, his body switching to autopilot and ignoring his orders. Chemicals and cravings raised the heat in Russs's blood and made his self-preserving good intentions fade to a hum in the back of his head. Sarah moved, a shifting of her legs that touched her knee to Russ's thigh. He swallowed and countered her movement with one of his own, a hand reaching out to cup her shoulder. A split second was all it took to decide—use that hand to keep her at arm's length or pull her closer. Russ's body made the decision, urging her nearer as he leaned in and pressed his mouth to hers. He got lost in the smell of her skin, the warmth of her lips on his, got lost in the power of the physical connection they'd shared before, the one he'd nearly managed to convince himself had been a dream.

For a moment he gave in, deepening the kiss, his mouth hungry and needy, desperate to feel this with her again and believe it had been there before, real all along. Then she touched him, a small, smooth hand on his neck—the tiniest seduction but one that hit Russ like a whip. He pulled away and set a hand on her collarbone, a drawbridge spanning the moat he'd built between them. He stared down at their knees.

"I can't," he said. "It's too soon. Or too ruined. I don't know...but I can't. Sorry."

He looked up as she licked her lips, regret painted all over her pretty face. She stood and took a step away from the couch and table, wrapping her arms around her middle. "I understand. I'm sorry too."

Russ flinched, her apologies still grating on him for all those reasons he didn't really understand. He got to his feet, avoiding her eyes. "I should let you get to bed, I guess."

He sensed her nodding in his periphery. Unsure what else to say, he grabbed a candle and left her be, closing himself in the bathroom. He stared at his reflection as he brushed his teeth, thinking he looked damn tired in the low light, closer to forty than thirty...which was true. But he hadn't really felt that way until today, after his first taste of new love and romantic excitement had been wrenched away as quickly as it'd come. He turned the tap to rinse his brush, only to realize again that the water was out with the electricity. He abandoned his toothbrush and self-analysis and headed to his room, hoping sleep would come to him quickly tonight.

With the fire still warming the room, Sarah lay down atop the blankets and watched the flames. She heard the bathroom door creak and closed her eyes as Russ exited and shut himself in his room. She wanted to go after him, but she'd overstepped her bounds far too much for one night already. She gave the pillow under her head a good punch, frustrated. Frustrated to have realized how hopeless a dream being with that man was, and frustrated deep in her body too, her selfish curiosities doomed to go unexplored. She imagined him now, changing out of his clothes and settling into his cold bed. If she'd been honest from the start, she might be in there with him, warming his stiff muscles and listening to his breaths quicken, tasting his mouth. She gave the pillow another slug.

Russ got under the bedspread in his chilly room, though he wondered if it might be wiser to stay cold—the discomfort might keep his body from pondering what his brain had just chosen to deny it. She was out there in the warm den, surely on that couch that had been forever changed since her arrival. Before her, merely a piece of inherited furniture, so familiar his eyes passed right over it. Now, practically a living thing, pulsing with memories. Her body, her voice, her hands and mouth on him...

Fuck it. He pushed his shorts down and fisted his cock, tight, as if he were punishing himself. He hated this hand, frankly, hated how lonely this felt after two brief but blissful nights in Nicole's—in Sarah's—arms. But he pictured her face, imagined her peeling away her shirt, stepping out of her jeans, pale slender legs against the leather of the couch.

Frustration unbearable, Sarah propped up her knee and slid her hand inside her panties, grazing the pads of her fingers across her clit. She'd feel like crap when this was over, but stung ego or not, she needed it. She wouldn't get any sleep until she gave herself a facsimile of what she craved. She pictured Russ's bare body and imagined him kneeling between her legs in his bed...his stiff cock ready and waiting, dying to give her the thing they'd been missing. Sexual pleasure could never fix what she'd done to him, but she wanted that, still—to make the most wonderful man she'd ever met feel good, as cared for and welcome as his very proximity made her feel. She imagined him sliding inside her, surrender written all over his handsome face.

Russ tried to picture how she'd look as he gave in and finally went there with her. They were romantic thoughts at first, images of that expression he was most used to seeing on her in bed. Then other ones crept in, her features full of the harsher things that stood between them...longing and frustration, a sharp edge of distrust. His chest tightened, knowing how it'd feel if this fantasy were real. Some glorious mix of desperation and regret, the sex just as forbidden and ill-advised as it was sweet and pure. The thought got his desire glowing hotter, simmering in the center of his body.

For a man who lived a steady and predictable existence, trusted his gut and followed its advice, Russ wanted to make a terrible mistake, just once. He wanted to go back and redo that kiss from ten minutes earlier, take it as far as she'd let him. He suppressed a moan as his hand sped. He wished his skin was softer, his palm as small as hers. He wished it *was* hers. He tried to mimic the way she'd touched him as he conjured her face, her mouth lowering as she leaned in close...but no. Nothing like a favor. Nothing that kept them on two different levels. He rearranged the fantasy, bringing her naked body right alongside his on the bed, tangling their legs. He stroked himself tight as he imagined pushing inside her.

She remembered how hot his hand had felt that first night they met, his warm palm on her bare skin when he'd tended to her injury and taken care of her. And other parts of him...she relived the memory of touching his cock for the first time, the smooth heat of him, the hard flesh, the shallow pitch of his breathing. But this time, the right name on his lips.

She slid her fingers inside, wishing they were him. Wishing he'd emerge from his room and tell her he'd changed his mind. No, *show* her he'd changed his mind, offer up proof that whatever they shared was stronger than her mistake or his anger. Hell, she'd take the anger. He could take all that out on her, and she'd accept it, eagerly. Russ's strong, selfish body looming above hers, demanding whatever it wanted. Beautiful. That kind face, tightened with a dozen fiery emotions, and his muscles lit by the waning fire. Enough aggression that she'd never have to apologize again, free to wake up beside him as an equal.

Russ heard his own low moan as the fantasy evolved and shut his mouth. He kicked the covers from his overheated body and welcomed the cool air, wishing for other sensations. Her nails clawing his skin, teeth grazing his shoulder. He pumped his fist and imagined being on top of her...such a dull position normally, but loaded for the two of them, should it ever happen again. She'd made him feel like a man for the first time in years—a male animal. He thought she liked that, liked all those impolite things he'd toned down for Beth. Well he wanted those things now. He wanted the harsh slap of skin on skin as their bodies came together, grasping hands and undignified noises and cursing. He wanted to wrap his fingers in her hair and taste her mouth, deep and rough. He wanted to feel every pound and inch of difference in their sizes, hear it in their voices, feel her soft wetness against his hard cock and feel like a man in the worst way.

She bit her lip to quiet her racing breaths as she imagined Russ giving in and losing himself right on top of her. She'd heard that three times now, the sound of him coming undone. But never inside her. The idea tightened her like a spring. Russ's face as he lost control of his body and succumbed to its wishes, thrusts fast and frantic—

—her hand on his hip, following the motions, the other on her clit as she chased his pleasure, raced him to the finish—

—that deep voice, deeper than she'd ever heard it, creeping toward crescendo alongside his excitement, her name, her actual name—

"Sarah."

"Russ." The whispered syllable came out pained as her body gave in, brain blank but for the memory of his strained face.

"Sarah." He repeated it again, then a last time, once for each spasm as his pleasure peaked and ebbed. Her eyes and mouth faded from his fevered mind and his body cooled. Russ stared into the darkness above his bed, listening to his own heart racing behind the sounds of the dying storm.

A whir, a beep. The power returned, a red 12:00 blinking to life from the bedside table. And just like that, reality intruded. Just like that, the ache returned to Russ's heart.

Chapter Ten

Sarah woke the next morning at sunrise, frustration still pacing in her chest. She sat up from her tangle of covers as Russ passed by, a cold breeze chasing him from the back door.

"Morning," she said through a yawn.

He offered a smile then began fiddling with the coffeemaker.

"I heard the power come back on before I fell asleep."

Russ didn't reply.

"Want me to make breakfast or anything?"

"That's all right."

"Okay." Looking around the room, she wondered what she'd do to fill her day. She suddenly missed her old routines in Buffalo. She missed running. She'd taken that up in junior high and clung to it as her release valve lest she ever get tempted to reduce her anxiety or get out of her head in any of the awful ways her mother had favored. Or the ways her former friend had, so many of the people she'd once gone to school with. She'd never chosen that route, yet here she was now, still burdened by the consequences of other people's actions.

She'd been on the run for nearly a month, high on adrenaline, but she still missed running of the meditative variety. Plus here it'd surely be even better, with no errant jerks loitering on the sidewalks, more than happy to toss an unwelcome flirtation her way.

Russ took a seat at the table as the coffee began burbling. He seemed tired this morning, and a bit distant. *Too ruined,* her head echoed.

He could probably use some space from her. The thought filled her with ice. Funny how she'd made a break for it just days ago, but now the thought of leaving terrified her. This place was safe, and she craved that. She was free here in some ways, or freer than she was on the outside, anyhow. Sanctuary. That's what this was. Still, fine line between a sanctuary and a cell.

"Russ?"

He looked up from his paper. "Mmmm?"

"I'd like to go out today. By myself."

His expression was tough to read. "Like take the truck out?"

"No. Just for a walk down the road or around the fields or wherever. I haven't really been alone for a while. And I know you haven't had a moment's rest from me, either. I mean, we both remember what happened last time you left me alone, so if you aren't okay with that yet, I get it."

He swallowed, unfocused gaze aimed out the window. "No, that's fine. Any idea when you'll be back?"

She shrugged. "An hour, maybe?"

He looked back to the page. "Have at it. The dogs will probably try to follow you."

"That's fine. I can handle canine company. And I can handle you too, of course, but I wouldn't mind a little space."

"You don't have to explain."

"Explanations are the least of what I owe you, Russ."

His nostrils flared with a deep inhalation, and his eyes rose to settle on hers. "It's fine. You don't owe me anything."

"Actually, I owe—"

"Enjoy your walk."

"Thanks."

Russ went back to his paper. "There's a trail around the perimeter of the property. We rode on it for a bit yesterday. It might be overgrown now, but it starts at the far end of the paddock and wraps all the way around, follows the edge of the woods, comes out on the road, maybe a quarter mile that way." He waved absently toward town.

"Cool. Thanks."

After a pit stop in the bathroom, Sarah drank a glass of water at the kitchen sink. She changed out of her jeans and into a pair of Russ's shorts, peeled away her long-sleeved shirt. She folded her clothes and set her wallet on top, in case Russ might appreciate some extra proof she didn't intend to run off.

He glanced up as she laced her sneakers at the door, taking in the boxers and camisole. "You're going walking in that? It's only about fifty-five out."

"Yeah. I might go for a bit of a jog. I'll warm up, don't worry. I've had worse in Buffalo."

"Right. Well, enjoy yourself."

She cast him a smile she hoped didn't look as sad as it felt, and exited through the storage and laundry room. She rubbed her goose-bumpy arms against the chill, patting each of the dogs as they trotted up.

"You guys like to run?"

One of them barked—Kit, she thought.

"Great. Let's see about that path."

Russ did his level best to not worry while Sarah was gone, but his heart was tight in his chest the entire forty minutes, eyes staring blankly at the local business news, taking nothing in. As the screen door creaked open and he heard her shoes drop onto the porch, he found himself able to breathe again. She pushed the inside door in, cheeks flushed, the hair around her face damp with sweat like the patches of her tank top beneath her arms.

"Well," he said. "Guess you warmed up just fine after all."

She nodded and smiled, still huffing faintly. "Yeah. I haven't been running in weeks, but that wasn't too bad. The dogs are recovering out back. I think I wore them out."

"How was the trail? Did you use it?"

"Yeah, it's great. Sort of wild in places, but pretty clear." She balanced on one foot and hugged the opposite knee to her chest. "It must be nearly three miles."

"Yeah, sounds about right."

"Can't say my legs did the run much justice. I was pretty rusty. Still, it felt good just to move."

"Good."

"You um..." She gulped a breath and switched the leg she was stretching. "It's really beautiful, your home. Your property, I mean. I know I've told you that before, but being out there just now... Anyhow, it's really something else. Thanks for letting me get out for a bit."

Russ nodded. His wife had carved that path through the grass over the course of a thousand morning walks. It'd grown over since she'd passed, and now a new woman was blazing a trail. Was that Russ's scab Sarah was ripping off or a wall she was tearing down? Spitting on Beth's memory or reviving it? Like he had the first clue. What he did know was that she might be running in circles now, but at least she wasn't running away.

He glanced at her feet then off toward the porch where her flimsy shoes had been left. "What size are your feet?"

"Eight, eight and a half. Depends. Why?"

"You shouldn't run in those sneakers of yours," he said. "They can't be good for your arches or your ankles."

"Probably not. Just tell me you don't plan to shoe me like a horse."

He folded his paper. "Next time I have a job to do near town, I'll swing by the shoe store and see if they have something cushier."

Her smile was warm and it lit Russ up from the inside.

"That's sweet, but running shoes are like bras. You can't grab a pair off the shelf and expect they'll fit right. And speaking of bras, this one's not exactly ideal." She plucked at the strap.

Russ swallowed, pushing away the knowledge of how she looked in said bra. "No, I guess not."

"But really, it was nice to even be moving like that again. Think it cleared out some of my cobwebs."

"Well, if you stick around, maybe we'll have to take a trip into Billings, see what we can find you at a mall. I've got some stuff I ought to stock up on too."

She nodded. "I'd like that."

"And actually, I was thinking..."

"Thinking about what?"

Russ cleared his throat, finally ready to voice the issue that had been dogging him since he'd remembered it upon waking. "A client of mine is retiring this week, and a bunch of folks are throwing a party for him at the bar tomorrow night."

Her warm smile curled at the edges, transforming to a smirk. "You need a designated driver?"

Russ shook his head. "More like a date." He held her eyes and watched them widen. "Not like, a date-date. As a friend. As my guest. I mean, I hope that's how you feel now. A guest, not a prisoner."

"I'm getting there... And yeah, I'd love to get out again. Out with you, I mean. I won't run."

Russ flinched, hating the dynamic that'd grown between them, this apologetic streak of tenuous trust. "I know you won't run."

"Only around and around in circles." She smiled and pointed out the window toward the fields.

He took a stab at joking back, praying they were ready for it. "For all I know you're in training for an epic escape act."

His heart sank for a few beats as she held her tongue, eyes narrowing. "And for all I know, you're going to drop me off at the sheriff's station on the way to this so-called party."

He nodded. "For all each of us knows."

Her smile returned, slow and sly. "Well do me a favor, Russ. Get a couple strong drinks in me before you turn my ass in. Send me off in style."

"There's a pretty good chance the sheriff could be at the going-away bash."

"Oh."

"But I mean, he wouldn't be looking for you. Not all the way out here."

Sarah frowned. "No, probably not. He can't memorize every federal wanted poster, I guess."

"It's a sleepy town, but no, I doubt even he's got that much free time..." He crossed his arms. "When's the last time you checked the internet, anyway? Do you know any details about the case, like if it's been on the news or anything?"

"I haven't checked it, actually."

He blinked. "Really?"

"Well, I checked the Buffalo news the day after I left town. I saw the story, just a blurb. 'Suspect wanted in drug-deal-gone-violently-wrong' or something like that, and the date and the address. I saw enough to know the cops were investigating it. The only other chances I've had to check were at a couple libraries, and I was afraid to Google anything specific and bring up a screen with my face plastered all over it with like a big wanted banner."

"Oh, right."

"Or to check my email, in case the feds can track that kind of thing. I don't know how it works. And I'm afraid to know, frankly."

"What if it's like, blown over? What if you're free to get back home?"

She shook her head. "Murders don't just blow over, Russ. Not even in *my* crappy neighborhood. Plus what am I supposed to go back to, even if everything were magically okay? I didn't leave a career or any family. I've got a few friends I'll miss, but way more enemies, now. Buffalo's over. I'm okay with that. I wanted to move on years ago, except I had no money and a mother I didn't trust to leave alone."

"Right."

She worked her fingers through her tangled hair. "But yes, I'd love to be your date or whatever. Too bad I don't have something nice to wear."

"The folks in town consider anything aside from overalls dressy. You'll be fine."

She nodded and Russ got lost in thoughts like those from the night before—visions of Sarah in a dress, shining like those women from her magazines.

"Well, I stink. I better take a shower."

He nodded, pushing that visual from his mind as well.

"And later I thought maybe I'd start going through your spare room. If that's okay with you."

"Yeah. Let me know when, and I'll try and give you some direction."

"Thanks again." She said it over her shoulder and her flushed face was transformed by a smile as she disappeared into the bathroom.

Russ turned to stare out the window across his field, imagining her running along the border, hair swinging, dogs chasing. "Seven years it takes you to find a woman you like," he muttered to himself. "Figures you'd pick the one with a price on her head."

Sarah rounded the side of the house as Russ's truck crunched up the gravel driveway in the early afternoon. He'd been called out for most of the morning on jobs and left her without enough chores. She'd thrown a stick for Kit for so long her elbow ached.

Russ returned her wave as he hopped out of the cab. Before he slammed the door, she spotted his keys dangling from the ignition and wondered if he'd done that consciously or not.

"Anything exciting?" she asked.

"No, not terribly. You?"

"Think I gave myself arthritis from playing fetch with your dog, but that's about it. Can I make you lunch?"

He shook his head. "Got fed on my last job."

"Oh, that's a nice perk."

Russ smirked. "I think this woman wants to betroth me to her daughter...but I won't turn down a free meal."

Sarah forced a smile. "You shouldn't turn down a free daughter, either, from the sound of the dating pool around here."

"Twenty's a bit young for me," he said, heading for the front porch.

How about twenty-seven? "If you have a few minutes to explain it, I'd love to start organizing your back room."

He kicked his boots off at the door and she followed suit.

"Yeah, no problem. Just let me change."

A few minutes later Russ emerged from his room in fresh clothes and poured himself a cup of cold coffee from the machine. "You um... You made my bed."

She held her breath.

"Thanks," he added.

Sarah exhaled. "I invented a bunch of things to do, actually. I hope you didn't have some special system worked out for your albums, because they're alphabetical by artist now."

Russ laughed, a sound she hadn't heard in far too long. "That'll do nicely."

"The W section's quite excessive."

Russ set his coffee on the dinner table and put his hands to his hips, looking her straight in the face. "Thank you."

"Not sure I deserve th—"

He put up a hand to cut her off. "Don't. If you apologize to me one more time my heart's going to break."

"Oh." She held back the "sorry" straining to follow that syllable.

"I know you're sorry. And you do deserve my thanks, for what you're doing around the house. I think you wish you could take back what happened those first few days as much as I do."

The theft or the sex?

"So let's just...let's just do that," he went on. "Let's try to forget how we started out."

"Okay."

"You just be Sarah, and I'll be me, and you're here to help out until you decide what comes next for you."

The invitation was kind, though it drove a nail into her chest to hear the situation's temporary status laid out so plainly. "I'd like that."

Russ stepped forward and shook her hand firmly. "Good. No more apologies for what happened."

"Agreed."

He nodded.

"Put me to work."

He picked up his cup and wandered past her to the back room, pushing the door in. It was a cheerful space, sunny, with the same view of the front yard as Russ's bedroom. Sarah took in a few items she hadn't noticed the previous night, a large wicker hamper filled with fabric beside an ancient Singer table, its attached sewing machinery flipped tidily into storage position. Her salivary glands kicked in. She walked over and ran a reverent hand over its dusty wood. "Wow."

"Yeah, my wife was into quilting."

"I hope you don't plan on selling this. It must be fifty years old."

"I always meant to bring it to her sister. I think it used to belong to their grandma."

Sarah nodded, still ogling.

"I'll be right back." Russ left and returned a minute later with a fistful of white trash bags and a Sharpie. Sarah snapped to attention.

"So to start, I'd like to get all the clothes out of the closet so I can take them to the Salvation Army drop-off. Anything that the moths got to you can put in another bag and label it trash."

"Okay."

"And I'm going to see if I can find the original box for that crib." He nodded to it. "I can't remember if it's tricky to take apart, but I'd like to get that donated too."

"Sure thing." She watched Russ's face as he poked around the tidy piles of stuff, expression blank. She'd given up on any number of aspects of her old life since arriving here, but it must feel different, giving up on hopes for parenthood...disassembling the dreams one had shared with now-missing loved ones. If Russ was hurting, he hid it well. He rummaged then slid a large flattened box from behind the bookshelf.

"Eureka." He leaned it against the wall, looking pleased. "Feel free to get to work on the closet. I'll figure out what tools we need for this."

We. Odd chore to share with the man she'd desperately wanted to sleep with. *Still* desperately wanted to sleep with, if she was honest. He'd put the kibosh on sex, and the intimacy inherent in helping pack away his abandoned potential for fatherhood and his dead wife's clothes was an absurdly unsatisfying substitute.

She sighed to herself. *He's your friend now, if you're lucky. Live with it.*

Sarah slid the closet door aside and took stock. Lots of sweaters and coats, a wooden shelf neatly lined with women's shoes. She grabbed a trash bag, flattening it against the floor then labeling it *donate*. She inventoried the hangers and tried to picture the woman who'd once worn these clothes. Practical, surely. A woman who favored wool in earth tones and comfortable, well-made size-seven leather shoes in a drab rainbow of browns and black. It was an ugly impulse to judge a person seven years dead as a rival, but it was a human impulse as well. Sarah allowed herself a few bitter thoughts about the woman who'd deserved a man as good as Russ as her husband. For one, she dressed like a matron, though she couldn't have been much older than thirty when she died. Sarah flicked through the hangers. Olive green, navy blue, maroon—

"Whoa." She slid it forward from the back of the closet— floor-length cream satin.

Russ walked over and joined her in staring at the gown. Sarah turned to find him smiling, not looking pained, merely thoughtful.

"Wow." Sarah ran a gentle hand down the fabric. "This is beautiful."

He nodded. "Her sister made it."

"Wow," she said again. "I know dresses, and this is, like, amazing."

"You know dresses?"

"Oh yeah. I love sewing." She lifted it from the closet and studied the seams, the darts, the detailing around the neckline. "Your wife must have had a beautiful figure." She couldn't have guessed it from the collection of shapeless sweaters. A size ten, the fitted top half of the dress suggested, slender but lush in the breasts and hips. "I always wanted curves." She gave the gown a final appreciative study and hung it up tenderly.

"She always wanted long legs," Russ said.

Sarah smiled, feeling a strange sensation of closeness, perhaps with Russ, perhaps with his dead wife. They'd shared a lover and a predictable set of female woes, coveting bits of each other's figures. The jealous curiosity left her, along with the sadness and the hopeless feeling that she'd never stack up to the woman he'd married, her perfection frozen in his memories.

"What was it like, your wedding?" she asked, still staring into the closet.

"Pretty simple. Sort of a glorified barbecue."

"Mighty nice gown for a barbecue."

"Well her sister lives for that stuff. Beth would've been happy in jeans."

She met his eyes. "That was her name? Beth?"

Russ nodded.

"You miss her?"

She studied his face as he thought and noticed new lines etching his brow, a pair of gray hairs at one temple.

"I missed her terribly for the first year or two. Then after a while, I think I missed women, in general. I'll always miss her, of course... I feel sad that she didn't get to be around longer, to have the kids she wanted. And I'm sad for her family. But I don't feel bad for myself anymore, not the way I used to."

"Was she like your soul mate, do you think?"

Russ made a quizzical face. "I don't know... She was my partner, was how I thought about it. We got along real well, shared the same priorities and politics, respected each other, liked each other's families. We made a lot of sense together. I loved her, a lot. And I'm pretty sure we'd have stayed married for the long haul, if we'd gotten the chance."

She could sense a "but" in his tone but didn't dare ask for details.

Russ cleared his throat. "Me and Beth weren't hot-blooded together, I guess I'd say. Steady, reliable, kind to each other. Loving, you know, but not crazy passionate."

"Ah." Sarah let an awkward silence hold court for a moment before she plowed onward. "I always went the other way. Gravitated toward the unreliable jerks who I figured my nonexistent dad would disapprove of."

"Like the bad-boy types?" Russ asked, a smile tugging the corners of his lips.

"Yeah, I guess you could say that."

"I must be like Dullsville, after all that. I mean, not that you and me..." He flicked a finger between them, trailing off with a faint pink glow in his cheeks.

Sarah laughed. "Are you kidding? I don't think you're dull. Heck, you're the most exotic guy I've ever been with, or whatever we were. Plus the deadbeats lose their appeal when you start sneaking up on thirty. And now, with my life all crumbled down around me, I could use all the stability I can get. So no, not dull. Quite a refreshing change of pace, in fact."

"I'll take it."

"What should...what do you want to do with it? The dress? If you keep it you should really get a garment bag for it."

"I think maybe I'll give that to Caroline as well. Beth's sister. Is that weird, a husband giving back his wife's dress?"

Sarah shrugged. "I have no idea what the etiquette is. But if she made it, I think that's okay. I mean, she'd understand if it was hard for you to hang on to it, right?"

It was Russ's turn to shrug.

"Ask her."

He nodded.

"Anyhow, I'll just leave it here for now." She slid it gently to the rear of the closet, exchanging an odd look with Russ before he turned back to his own thoughts and projects.

Sarah glanced at the shiny satin every few moments as she finished sorting the clothes, thinking it looked a hell of a lot like a ghost, hanging there. After she cinched the third and final trash bag she pulled it from rack and walked to the other side of the room, hooking the hanger onto a nail that held a wall calendar, trapped on July from seven years earlier.

Russ looked up from his toolbox, staring at the dress, then her face.

"It felt wrong, leaving it in there by itself," Sarah said, fluffing out the skirt.

He smiled tightly.

"If you're going to give it back, you should let it enjoy a few more days or weeks of the limelight first."

Russ pursed his lips, expression going cold.

Sarah felt her own mood plummet. She thought the gesture had been a kind one, an open show of deference.

With quick, controlled movements, Russ quietly put his tools away and left the room.

"Russ?"

No reply.

She followed him into the den. "Russ?"

He'd braced his hands on the arm of the loveseat and was leaning over, head hung.

"Are you okay? I didn't—"

"Don't, please." He stood up straight and rubbed his face. "Jesus."

"I don't understand what I did."

He turned to look at her. "You changed, okay?"

Her heart sank. "Of course I did. I was lying before, about who I really am." Clearly he didn't like who she actually was.

Russ pinched the bridge of his nose and shut his eyes, looking every one of his thirty-six years and then some. He swallowed and blinked at her.

"What?"

"When you first showed up," he began, then trailed off. "Hell, I don't even know how to explain it."

"Well try, please."

"It was like... For the first time in forever, a woman waltzed into my life. An eligible woman, who seemed to want me as much as I wanted her. It made me feel like a man again—a whole one. Not a widower to handle like he's still mourning, or a warden, or someone wronged who had to be apologized to, over

168

and over again. Those first couple days you looked at me in this way no one's done in years."

"Like someone who didn't already know you."

He nodded, breaking their eye contact.

Sarah swallowed. "I know how that feels." She listened to Russ's deep inhalations and gathered her thoughts. "You're the first person I've met in ages who didn't know me as my mother's daughter, or my exes' ex, or as a nameless female body behind a bar." She stared at his socks for a moment then met his gaze. "My history sucks, Russ. I was a decent kid, really, but when your mom was into the bad stuff mine was, it's like everyone's just waiting for you to turn rotten too, even yourself. You're the first person I've gotten to know in ages who didn't see me as a screw-up in school or the daughter of an addict. Then I wrecked that...and now you've offered it to me again. I've never had a clean start like that. I used to fantasize that my dad would turn up and move me away to another city, where I could reinvent myself as whatever I wanted. Being here was like a little taste of that. And if I could, I would have changed my name to Nicole in a heartbeat if it meant I could start over and be with somebody as nice as you."

Russ made a noise, a laugh with no joy filling it. He stepped to the front of the loveseat and sank into the worn cushions. For nearly a full minute he didn't speak, then he finally looked up. "I'm not as nice as you think I am."

"You are." She slid a chair over from the table to sit a few feet from him.

"I wasn't, just now. You're helping me out and I just snapped at you for no good reason."

She shrugged.

Russ stared down at his hands clasped between his knees. Sarah realized for the first time he didn't wear his wedding ring anymore. Had she noticed it that first morning, she'd have guessed it was because the memory pained him too much. Now she knew better. He didn't wear it because he was done being a formerly married man and saw himself as what he was—single. Widower and drug addict's daughter, they'd both been saddled with pitiable labels through no fault of their own. He got handled with undue care, her with suspicion.

"I don't see you that way," she said quietly. "I promise."

Russ kept his eyes on his hands.

"I hate feeling like I'm being looked at and put into some category. I don't look at you that way either. I just see you. And all this." She waved her hand around to indicate his home, this little parcel of endangered America.

Russ smiled. "Hope you don't mean the interior decorating."

Her heart melted, body relaxing. "I know you're secretly stuck in the forties with your cowboy record collection, not the seventies with your orange and avocado decor."

"Good. Anyhow...sorry about before. I know I asked you to stop apologizing for everything. Maybe I should make a decision to stop looking for invisible messages in how you treat me."

She nodded. "I wouldn't mind that."

They stood, and for the second time that day, they shook hands.

"I better tend to the horses," Russ said, looking out the back window. "If you feel like it, the crib comes apart with an Allen wrench. Should be one that fits in my toolbox."

"Sure thing."

"Oh and I got a call from a friend about the party tomorrow. If you still feel like going, I figure we should head out around six thirty. We can eat there."

"I'm sure I'll want to go."

He offered a smile, tired but warm. "I look forward to it. We'll have to think up a good story on the drive into town."

"Mail-order bride?"

Russ laughed. "Better get to work on your Russian accent, Natasha."

"Will do."

"That is, if the sheriff's deputy hadn't already met you when we were parked at the station the other day. He'll be there, I'm sure."

"Foiled again."

She watched him shrug on his coat by the back door and exit with a wave. She didn't have the faintest idea what he was to her anymore—host under duress, ruined lover, friend of a decidedly Stockholm variety. She didn't really care. Russ had decided to take her at her word after she'd done nothing to deserve his trust, offering her a kind facsimile of the blank slate she'd been craving her entire life.

Beyond the window and the yard, he led Mitch out into the pen, dogs at his heels. Some handsome stranger. Some broken kind of perfect.

Chapter Eleven

When Russ got home the next day from his morning appointments, he felt calm. For the first time since the betrayal, he harbored no fear as he turned into his driveway, and entertained no worries that Sarah could have disappeared in his absence. They'd reached something not unlike a truce, but not exactly identical to one. An understanding, or the mutual desire to understand one another.

He left his keys in the ignition and slammed the door. Buoyed at the thought of there being someone inside to greet him as he entered, he gave the dogs a good tussle then jogged up the steps with a new energy. But instead of Sarah's voice or smile, his entrance was met by a strange chugging sound, familiar but long forgotten. As he set his case by the door, he placed the noise—the sewing machine. He walked to the door of the back room, as filled now with sunshine as it had been filled with the gristle of tough memories yesterday. Sarah was seated at Beth's old Singer, the needle gobbling blue fabric from under her fingers. Russ knocked on the threshold.

She glanced up, surprised. "Hey."

"Hey yourself. Guess that old thing still works."

She nodded and adjusted the needle. "You said the fabric was okay to donate, so I hope it's okay that I used it."

"Absolutely. What are you up to?"

"I'll show you." She stood, curling her finger as she passed by to lure him back into the den. She walked to the couch then gestured like a spokesmodel at the picture window, one of Russ's faded, orange drapes replaced with a length of blue.

He nodded his approval. "Very nice. But it'll make the rest of the decor look that much worse."

"It's a start." She ran her hand over the fabric, fussing with the way it fell. "If I end up staying all winter and I manage to fix up one or two things a week, you'll have a new home by spring."

"Well, I'm very impressed." He joined her in admiring her handiwork, and considered the fabric. Beth had picked that out, intending it for someone's Christmas quilt, maybe. She was gone but here was a little taste of her, decorating the room. Russ liked that. It felt exactly how he wanted his memories of his wife to—not hidden away, but not locked in a time capsule, either. Modified and included, enriching this home instead of haunting it. His body warmed from the floor up and a smile overtook his face. Then an idea struck. Inspiration.

"You eat lunch already?"

She nodded.

"Good. Get your shoes on."

"Why? Where are we going?"

"On a road trip."

Sarah studied Russ's face as he turned them onto the road. He'd refused to tell her where they were going, but she didn't mind. There was something playful about him just now, a boy with a secret. She relaxed back into the passenger seat and let him transport her.

Friends. They were friends again. The previous evening had been ample proof. After their talk, Russ had shed an invisible weight. She'd finished in the back room, and they'd cooked dinner and worked on the puzzle for a couple of lazy hours, listening to his old records. He'd told her some of his great-grandfather's war stories, a taste of his family's modest yet rich history. The way he'd perked up while sharing those details had taken the edge off her guilt for having attempted to steal a piece of said history. The only part of the evening that saddened her was the lack of sexual tension. She still felt that gnawing attraction, but last night Russ had seemed free of it. Now, too. She stole at a look at his eyes, those pale greenish irises lit up even as he squinted against the sun.

When he turned them onto a new route and the sign for a highway announced they were heading toward Billings, Sarah caught on.

"You're taking me shopping."

Russ merely smiled.

"Wow. Thank you. A lot."

"We'll be a little late for the party, but that's fashionable, right?"

She nodded. "I um... I'll have to borrow money from you."

"I owe you for all the work you did on that room yesterday. I'll pay you off in sneakers and some new clothes."

Sarah remembered a favorite movie from her teenage years—*Pretty Woman.* It sort of rang true. She was pretty down-and-out, though she was no prostitute. And Russ was no millionaire. But Sarah would happily take the mall and a party at a bar in place of Rodeo Drive and a fancy business dinner. She rolled with the comparison and let herself feel treated, not indebted. Who knew—maybe he'd overlook her circumstances and fall madly in love with her.

It was a long drive, nearly two hours. After miles of nondescript farmland, they reached the city limits and Russ asked, "What sort of stores do you need to go to?"

"Well, I guess a shoe store, for the sneakers. For clothes...anywhere, really. I'm not feeling very fussy."

Russ cruised along a main drag punctuated by a few big box stores.

"Oh, there. That's perfect." Sarah pointed to a discount designer shoe warehouse, and Russ turned them into the gigantic parking lot.

A thrill ran through her like electricity. Sarah wasn't a shopaholic, but this seemed so wondrous after nearly a month on the run. As the doors slid open to welcome them, she felt miraculously normal. Just any other woman, on the hunt for a perfect pair of sneakers.

Beside her, Russ made a *hmmm* noise.

"Yeah?"

His gaze jumped around the store. "This could take a while, right?"

"I'll try to be quick."

"No, don't be. Is it okay if I head to hardware store while you shop? I could meet you back here in a half hour."

The thought of Russ leaving her triggered a fearful pang, but she shrugged it off. "Yeah, perfect."

"Great. Much as I love shoes..." Again, his eyes took in the endless aisles, probably as dull to him as the hardware store would be to her.

She waved toward the exit. "Away with you."

"Listen... Find some running shoes, but look for some boots too. For when it gets nasty out. And something for tonight, for the party."

She bit her lip. "That sounds like too much."

Russ shrugged, downplaying his generosity. "If you stay all winter you'll have plenty of time to pay me back."

She nodded, thinking it over. "Okay. Thanks."

"See you in thirty minutes."

"Bye." She watched until he disappeared into the sunshine then turned her attention to the orgy of choice. She tackled the sneaker issue first, finding a quality pair that suited her arches and her aesthetics. Boots were tough. The current, sexy knee-high styles tried to seduce her, but Sarah selected a practical waterproof pair. She wondered what Russ had in mind when he'd told her look for shoes for the party. Surely not heels. She wandered up and down the dress-shoe aisles, feeling high from all the colors and materials—a magazine spread come to life here before her. How had she ever treated shoe shopping as something to do to blow time before? Now it felt like a luxury, a trip to an amusement park. She savored every moment, drinking in the patterns and textures and the smell of new leather and rubber.

By the time Russ found her, she'd settled on a pair of red velvet flats, not terribly well made, but marked to sell and cute as all-get-out. Russ didn't ask the price of anything, simply went with her to the checkout and paid, carrying her bags to the truck.

"Thanks again," she said.

"You're welcome."

"You should give me the receipt, so I can keep track of what I owe you."

Russ stowed her purchases in the back of the cab and they climbed inside. "I'll stick it to the fridge, how about that?"

"Yeah, okay."

"Where to next?" he asked.

"I guess I could use some clothes...so a mall with all the usual chain stores, or one of those big Kohl's-type places. Even Target's fine."

"I think there's something like that just up the street." Russ drove them back onto the road, and she wondered if he noticed what she did—the bus station. The last place she'd slept before

Russ took her in. Shame gnawed at her nerves. She held her breath, convinced for a moment that he was going to pull in and give her the boot. But they cruised right on by and sure enough, there was a Kohl's only two blocks away.

"Perfect."

"How long do you need? I want to swing by a feed store, a ways outside of town. Is two hours too long?"

She laughed. "Two hours to shop sounds like heaven."

"Great. Let's see..." Russ dug his wallet out again and counted out bills. "Is a hundred and forty enough for some new outfits?"

"Oh God, that's plenty."

"Well here, take it." He handed her the twenties. "If there's anything left over, that's a bonus."

"Wow. Okay." As she folded the bills and slid them into her pocket, a scary thought flashed across her mind. He was giving her this money because he wasn't coming back. For a second the cab seemed to close in on her, then she swallowed and got herself together. "Where should I meet you?"

"I couldn't say exactly when I'll be back, so I guess I'll just try to find you in the store."

She nodded.

"I'll aim for two hours, but it may be a bit longer."

"Cool. Perfect."

Russ searched her face. "Everything okay? You look sort of...stressed out."

"No, I'm just a little overwhelmed. It's weird to be doing something this normal again."

"I'll bet."

"See you in a couple hours."

"Have fun."

She climbed out of the truck and waved as he drove off. *Please come back.* Please let this store's proximity to the bus depot be a coincidence.

But no, Russ wouldn't do that. He was a man of his word if ever she'd met one. Still, the fear dogged her as she entered the store. For the first half hour, she couldn't concentrate. She touched pretty items but couldn't focus enough to really comprehend what they were.

He wouldn't have bought you all those shoes if he didn't plan on bringing you back home.

His home, not yours.

But he didn't give me the receipt. Maybe he's planning to return them.

You're being irrational. He's the one who's worried you'll run off when his back's turned, remember?

Finally, her brain reached its capacity for worry and switched gears. She poured all her attention into the racks, got lost in them like a pleasurable, colorful labyrinth. After what felt like two hours, she carried her carefully selected items to the register, praying the sales tax wouldn't push her over her budget.

As it turned out, Montana was one of those renegade states that didn't do sales tax, and she accepted her receipt with nearly twenty dollars to spare.

The clerk handed over her bag, heavy with jeans and sweaters and underwear.

"Thanks. Do you have the time?"

The woman consulted the register. "Ten past five."

"Thanks." Shit, that was ten minutes over the two hours Russ had estimated. *Two hours or more,* she reminded herself. No reason to panic. She took a seat on a bench by the entrance and flipped through her new clothes. She'd wear the velvet shoes and patterned blouse and a new pair of jeans tonight to the party.

If he comes back, her brain reminded her.

She muttered "Shut up," to herself just as a mother and child came through the sliding doors, cold outside air enveloping Sarah as they passed. She watched them heading for the kids' section, envying how normal they were. Envying how boring that woman perhaps found her own life.

"Hey."

She jumped, shocked to find Russ standing to her left. "Hi!" she said, way too loud.

He laughed. "Did I scare you? I've been wandering around for almost fifteen minutes. It's like a hall of mirrors in here."

"You didn't scare me. I was just off in another world."

"Find some good stuff?" He opened the bag beside her on the bench and peered inside.

"Yeah, thanks. And I have your change."

Russ seemed to hesitate before accepting the bills she dug from her pocket. "Eighteen bucks..." He scanned the store.

"What?"

"Have you um... Did you decide what you're wearing tonight? To the bar?"

"Yeah. Nothing too fancy."

Russ wandered away and she followed, confused. He led her to the jewelry department, glass cases of more upscale rings and bracelets, cheaper costume stuff hanging along the partitions.

"Why don't you pick out something to go with it?" Russ suggested, browsing.

She felt a blush rise in her cheeks. "This trip was really about practical things. I don't want to spend your money—I mean, my future wages—on something silly. Four bucks for that stupid magazine was wasteful enough."

"What color are you going to wear?" Russ asked, eyes still preoccupied with the necklaces and earrings.

"The top's sort of patterned...red and fuchsia and gray. But I really—"

"What about something like this?" Russ plucked a necklace from its hook, red and pink beads.

"That's pretty, but it's a bit too matchy-matchy. Plus like I said, I don't need any jewelry."

Russ met her eyes. "Just let me, okay?" No challenge this time, merely a kind request, a favor being asked, even.

She sighed and submitted. Taking a slow inventory of the cheaper jewelry, she found a necklace made of three wire strands of crystal beads. "This is very nice." She scanned for a salesperson before sneakily unclasping it from its tag and trying it on. Checking her reflection in a cheap, wavery plastic mirror, she decided it was indeed beautiful. Russ stood just behind her shoulder, and suddenly this twelve-dollar necklace was worth more to her than that diamond-and-ruby monstrosity Richard Gere had given to Julia Roberts. She placed her palm to it, overcome for a moment.

"I like it," Russ said.

She met his gaze in the reflection. "Me too."

He left her and she studied herself a moment longer.

"There's earrings," Russ said and she turned to find him holding them up. Before she could decide whether or not to protest, he was walking toward the registers, his stride telling her the earrings would be leaving the store with them. She took the necklace off and followed.

Sarah watched the same clerk who'd helped her earlier checking Russ out. Like, *checking him out.* She didn't mind. In fact, Sarah followed suit, studying him as he made small talk and paid. So handsome. Not movie-star handsome—the kind of looks that conked a girl over the head—but the sort that if a woman were attracted to the type of man Russ was, she couldn't help but melt. And he wasn't Sarah's type, even, but she melted all the same. She was a lump of chocolate and Russ was a warm radiator. The longer she lingered near him, the gooier she felt. It felt nicer than getting conked over the head by some stunning man's looks. Far nicer by miles.

The horses weren't impressed to be kept waiting an extra half hour for their nightly attention, but Russ didn't let them guilt him. The trip had made him feel better than he had in ages, and not in the over-excited, desperately hopeful way he had when he and Sarah had first messed around. He just felt plain old satisfied. He finished putting the animals to bed and headed inside.

Sarah was standing in the den when he entered, and he had to stop and stare at her. She'd done her makeup again, pulled half her hair up into some style he had no word for. Her jeans were new—dark and stylish—and she had on her Christmas-y shoes and a colorful collared shirt. The necklace he'd bought her looked like snowflakes or diamonds scattered across her collarbone, matching beads dangling from her ears.

"Wow."

She laughed and looked down, checking out her feet in their new shoes. "It's not like I'm wearing a ball gown."

"I know, but still. You look..."

She nodded. "I look like me on a good day. I look like the old me, I guess. As a brunette."

Russ turned that around in his head. The "old" Sarah wasn't the type of woman he'd ever imagine would want to be with a man like him. Not a glamour queen or anything, but perhaps the sort of woman who required a man with a certain amount of urbane charm. Russ had never even tried sushi or ridden on a subway. He didn't know the names of any bands from after he'd graduated high school.

"What?" she asked, addressing his prolonged study.

"You look real nice, that's all. Wish I had something nicer to wear, so you wouldn't show me up so bad."

"I'm wearing jeans."

"Yeah, but those jeans aren't like the jeans we wear around here. You're gonna look like a celebrity."

She laughed. "Maybe that can be our cover story."

"Maybe... Well, I better get cleaned up. Party's probably started already."

Sarah took a seat on the couch and turned her attention to the puzzle.

Closing himself in his room, Russ felt his stomach growl, only a fraction of it the fault of an overdue dinner. A larger fraction was fear, irrational worry that Sarah might somehow have her cover blown when they ventured into town. But that was extremely unlikely. No, by far the biggest hunk of his anxiety came from simply being out with her, not knowing what to tell people they were. He was stuck with the lie he'd told Jim now, pretending she was here because of an interest in horses. That he could deal with. It was how to introduce the pair of them that made him itchy.

They weren't lovers anymore, and he certainly couldn't claim she was his girlfriend. That left her open to get flirted with by other men, a thought that made Russ's clothes feel suddenly stifling. He unbuttoned his shirt and swapped it for a clean one and changed into fresh jeans. He switched the light off and wandered to the den.

"Almost ready. Just need to shave."

She frowned. "No you don't."

"No?"

"No way. You look sexy all unshaven. Women love that."

"Do they?"

She shrugged. "I do, anyhow. And probably all the rugged ladies around here too."

He ran a palm over his stubbly chin, remembering with an unwholesome sexual pang what had happened the last time he'd shaved. "Well, I can use all the help I can get. Fine. Let's head out before whatever food they're providing gets gobbled up."

She rose from the couch and Russ noticed her face again, the makeup and the darker hair making her look dramatic in hard-to-pinpoint ways. He made a terrible mistake and imagined that hair spread out across his white pillowcase.

He cleared his throat. "You look real nice."

She laughed, glancing down at her clothes. "So you keep saying. You're probably just as sick of that other outfit as I am."

He looked to the couch and the floor, all the places those familiar garments had once been scattered. "You ready?"

"Yup."

Russ got his shoes on at the door and led her to the truck, opening her side first. He started up the engine in the freshly fallen darkness. It had been years since he'd done this—what felt like a date.

"We should figure out our story," he said. "And I think we need to at least stick with what I told Jim, about you being named Sarah and interested in horses. A stranger comes to town once in a blue moon here, so you're bound to be the most interesting thing to gossip about." *Especially to the men.* "The sheriff and Ben—his deputy—could already have traded notes on you."

"Where should I be from?"

He considered it as he turned them onto the road. "I'd normally suggest Buffalo, to keep things simple, but I guess we better err on the side of caution." Russ smirked to himself, probably unseen in the low light. He'd never in a million years have seen it coming, but taking part in this conspiracy with the most dangerous woman he'd ever met was just a tiny bit thrilling. "You said you always wanted to start over, and I guess this is your chance. Where'd you always want to be from?"

"Florida," she said without hesitation. "I always wanted to be from Florida. Orlando."

"Good. So you're Sarah from Orlando."

"Sarah Roberts," she added. "I thought Julia Roberts was the most glamorous woman alive when I was little."

"Easy enough. So, Sarah Roberts from Orlando, Florida, what made you develop an interest in horses at the ripe old age of twenty-seven? You talk to anybody for three seconds in this town, and they'll realize you're clueless, so we need a good reason why you're suddenly so keen."

She was silent a couple of minutes, thinking. "Well...I've been a bartender for a long time, in Florida. For a resort. And after all those years in the tidy tourist industry, I started craving something more rugged and smelly."

"Okay, I'm buying that."

"And I was friends with someone who was in charge of taking care of the horses that draw the carriages around the parks, with like Cinderella riding in them. They turned me on to it."

"I'm impressed. That sounds half-plausible."

"And the rest stays the same," Sarah said. "I left town at the end of the summer with my meager savings, came west and met you by chance."

"How did we meet?"

She considered it a moment. "I looked up horse vets in Montana, and you were nice enough to talk to me on the phone, give me advice about schools and invite me to come stay for a while, to do chores for you and decide if I like it."

Russ smiled, ready to believe the story himself. "Seems solid. And yeah, the rest can stay the same, really. What we've been up to, minus the night you made a run for it."

"Good, that's settled, then... I wonder if either the deputy or the guy from the dairy place will wonder why I changed my hair color."

"Men aren't too bright about stuff like that," Russ offered. "I only noticed your hair because it stank up my bathroom."

"Oh, thanks very much."

The warm banter had returned to them, and Russ had to stifle an urge to reach out and touch her—squeeze the nape of her neck or her shoulder, a small taunt to reinforce how familiar she felt to him.

"So," she said. "You and me are strictly mentor and student as far as everybody's supposed to know?"

Russ stared straight ahead at the road. "Yeah, I s'pose that's easiest." Easy as a bullet to the heart.

"So we're leaving two parts out, then. Me running away, and us...you know. Hooking up."

Hooking up. Damn, that stung. An accurate description, but ouch. "Yeah, that'd be the simplest story, don't you think?"

"Yeah."

Neither spoke for the rest of the trip and the glare of streetlights pulled Russ from a driving trance as they reached town. The bar's parking lot was already close to full, a predictably good turnout. Any excuse to get drunk for socially acceptable reasons lured the crowds from their sleepy weeknight routines. Russ recognized the deputy's cruiser and Jim's green truck as he parked. He steeled himself.

"Wow, it's noisy," Sarah said, unstrapping her belt.

"Yeah. Farmers and ranchers drink hard." Russ pocketed his keys and they headed for the entrance. He wondered how much of this weird feeling in his chest was nerves, and how much was pride for turning up with best-looking woman this bar had ever seen. He'd been proud to turn up here with Beth, too, of course. She'd been plenty pretty herself, but get a beer or two in her, and she'd curse a blue streak, slap your back just as hard as any man there and spew country war stories with the best of them. But Sarah was something exotic in her stylish and unmistakably not-from-these-parts clothes, lipstick instead of ChapStick, her figure not molded to a shape of broad, hardy sturdiness like most of the women from around here. Russ didn't know what to make of her himself as he held the door open, a ruckus greeting them.

"Thanks," she said, the word nearly lost to the music and laughter.

Russ waved to a couple of people then led Sarah toward the bar. "Get you something to drink?"

"A beer's fine."

He nodded, muscling his way through a small sea of acquaintances to shout for two bottles. He glanced to his sides, every man suddenly seeming like a threat. He hoped a couple drinks would soothe that sensation.

When the beers appeared, he pulled a fifty from his wallet and handed it to Harry, the regular bartender and the town's one and only black resident. "For whatever lucky souls come next," Russ said, and took the bottles. "Minus a few generous tips."

"Will do, doc."

"You seen Frank around?" Russ asked, scanning the crowd for the man of the hour.

"Near the juke."

"Thanks." He turned from the counter to find Sarah already beset by her first admirer, Ben. Russ had always thought the town's deputy was a bit annoying and a touch too swaggery, but seeing the way he stood now, thumb hooked behind his belt all cocky...that irritation snowballed into a full-blown grudge.

"Heya, Ben," Russ offered, handing over Sarah's beer. "You remember my friend."

Ben gave Sarah way too eager a grin. "I do indeed. Just asked her how that breakfast turned out."

Russ blinked.

"At the diner," Sarah prompted Russ. "After we left the station's parking lot?"

"Oh right. Yeah, just great."

"Best in town," Ben said grandly, eyes narrowing for a fraction of a second. "Where'd you say you were from again?"

"Florida."

"Oh yeah? You—"

Russ barged in. "You wanna meet the guest of honor?" he asked Sarah.

"Frank's a bit..." Ben mimed a drinky-drinky motion with an invisible bottle.

"Better catch him soon, then." Russ led Sarah away by the arm.

"Don't act too paranoid," Sarah muttered as they walked.

Paranoid? He wished. This was good old-fashioned jealousy. "Thought I was rescuing you. Ben can be kind of..."

She laughed. "Kind of what?"

"Flashy."

"He did go a bit cowboy on me," she said. "And he reeks of smoke, so thank you."

Russ smiled to himself, edging between a group of farmhands to tap Frank on the shoulder.

Frank turned, and his weathered face lit up with glassy, drunken happiness. "The good doctor! How you doin', Russ? Who'zis?" he added, spotting Sarah.

"This is Sarah," Russ said and watched Frank assault her hand with a very thorough shake. "She's staying with me for a bit, figuring out if she wants to study equine medicine."

"Oh yeah?"

Sarah nodded politely.

"What'd y'do before?" Frank asked, attempting to prop an elbow atop the jukebox but missing.

"Bartender," she said, and quickly added, "In Orlando."

"Oh yeah?" Frank's brows bobbed up. "Big city, huh?"

"I guess you'd say that."

"You prolly know all sorts of fancy cocktails then, huh? Martinis and them things with the cherries and umbrellas'n all that?"

"Sure. All sorts."

"Well, le's see it! Mix me up a fancy party drink." Frank swept an arm toward the bar and Sarah's eyes widened in tandem with Russ's.

"Oh, I couldn't," she said. "I don't know if my license covers Montana—"

"Nonsense! Nobody cares about that here."

Russ thought about protesting as Frank dragged her off by the elbow, but decided against it. If she was sticking around a bit, she might as well get used to the townspeople, and Frank was harmless enough. Russ followed them and watched Frank lift up the gate to the bar and usher Sarah inside.

"She's a bartender too!" he shouted to Harry.

Harry looked game. He owned the place and had no angry boss to answer to if he bent the rules. "Whereabouts?"

Frank answered for her. "Big city! Sunny Florida! I wanna see her make me some big fancy cocktail with an even fancier name."

Sarah and Harry exchanged a look, then Harry stepped aside to fill a few beer orders, leaving her to it.

She thought a minute, and Russ saw her go into pro-mode. "How about a Dirty Silk Panties?" she asked Frank, face completely straight.

He hooted and slapped the counter. "Bring it on!"

Sarah inventoried the shelf. She set a large shot glass on the bar and filled a shaker with ice and vodka and some other thing Russ didn't catch. She strained the concoction into the glass and dripped in some grenadine. Clamping her hand over the lip, she looked Frank square in the eye. "You've got a ride, right?"

Frank pointed in the direction of his wife, sipping a Coke by the door amid a gaggle of women.

"Super. Cheers." She slid the drink over.

Frank took a thoughtful sip, then downed the rest, returning the glass with an almighty *ahhh* of approval. "Another."

"You should let that one sink in first," she said.

"One for the good doctor, then." Frank clapped Russ hard on the back.

"I'm driving. And I've barely started this." Russ held up his beer bottle and fished in his wallet for a five to cover Frank's dirty panty drink.

"Fine then." Frank turned to the crowd and shouted "Hey!" at the top of this lungs. People quieted enough for him to announce, "We got a newcomer! Bartender from Florida. Come and see what this little lady can do! Any drink you ever heard of, I bet."

Russ looked to Sarah, and she didn't look fazed in the least by being treated like a carnival sideshow. She exchanged a look with Harry, who put his hands out to say his bar was her bar. Russ rankled for a moment, hoping he wasn't about to lose her company for the rest of the evening. But she looked intrigued by the chance. Happy, if he wasn't mistaken. She must miss this kind of chaos after leaving it behind to wake up in Russ's quiet world. He leaned in to address Harry. "You cut her some tips."

"Naturally. Your girl about to show me up in my own bar?" Harry asked with a grin.

Russ forced a smile. "She ain't mine, but yeah, I think maybe you're in trouble."

"Ain't yours, huh?" Harry's eyes darted to Sarah, and even though the man was two decades out of her league and the innuendo harmless, Russ felt a hot little spark prickle up his neck nonetheless.

"Just friends," Russ said firmly, knowing he had to get that straight in his own head sooner or later. Sarah met his eyes a second after he said it, face unreadable. "Don't let them monopolize you all night."

She grinned. "Only until I've earned all those new clothes." She turned to the crowd. "Who wants a Long Slow Screw?"

Chapter Twelve

At a quarter to ten, Sarah counted up the tips Harry handed her. Eighty-eight bucks would do very nicely. Not enough to cover all her new debts, but it'd pay off her sneakers and flats. She pocketed the bills and ducked away before anyone else could ask for a refill. It seemed as though she'd met the entire town, and been flirted with shamelessly by every male on the premises. Every male but one. She spotted Russ by the door, still nursing his second beer, and chatting with a couple about his age whose names she'd forgotten in the melee of glasses and orders and register math. They bid Russ a good-night and exited just as she reached him.

She tapped his shoulder, and he turned, looking surprised—looking as if he didn't recognize her for a few seconds.

"They let you go, then?" he asked, and took a sip of his beer.

"I escaped, more like."

"Sorry about that. Frank can be a force of nature when he's got a few in him."

"It was fun to be back behind a bar again. Plus I can put a nice dent in my I.O.U. Though your deputy sure gave me the third-degree. I'd have worried he was onto us, if he hadn't been so clearly preoccupied with my chest the whole time."

Russ nodded.

"I promised somebody I'd play pool with them." She craned her neck to see if the tall man in question was still around. She turned back to Russ. "Unless you're dying to head home?"

He shook his head. "Night's still young."

"Well you come play with me, then, until what's-his-name turns up. I don't see him just now."

Russ followed her to the worn-out table, and she fed it the quarters she'd collected from the register. "You any good at this?" she asked Russ.

"Not really. You?"

"I'm okay." The kind of "okay" one garnered over the course of a thousand quiet winter nights in a Buffalo bar. She racked the balls tidily and rolled the cue ball across the green felt to Russ.

"Ladies first," he said, stepping away.

"Alrighty." She found a stick and a chalk from a rack on the near wall, then leaned over and took aim. She broke the balls with a sharp crack, colors scattering, the three disappearing down the side pocket. "Solids."

Russ blinked at the table.

She sank five more balls in four turns, a small crowd gathering. She scratched a tricky shot and handed Russ the cue ball.

"I am so royally screwed," he said.

"Got that right," a nearby partygoer agreed.

Sarah smiled to herself, feeling at home for the first time in weeks. Usually when she kicked a guy's ass at pool, the satisfaction came from annoying him, taking him down a peg. With Russ it was much nicer than that. This was her good-natured revenge for watching him do what he did so effortlessly around the horses and the property, a little taste of who she was on an imitation slice of her home turf. It was also a welcome chance to watch Russ lean over. She gave his ass an appreciative glance as he took aim and sank a stripe.

"Very nice."

He straightened and fixed her with a falsely snide grin. "Don't patronize me, city girl."

"Don't give me a reason to, cowboy."

He shook his head and set up another shot, missed. The men in the crowd gave him a good razzing.

Sarah effectively played the rest of the game on her own, calling the corner pocket and sinking the eight. Russ clapped along with everyone else.

She smiled at him as she twisted her stick into the chalk cube. "Rematch?"

"Not on your life. Where's Tyler? He'll give you a run for your money."

The name jogged her memory. "Oh, he's the one who challenged me earlier. Really tall?"

"He went for a smoke," somebody said. "Think he just came back inside."

Russ made a beckoning motion with his arm. "Get him over here. He's our town's only hope for saving some face here. Hey, Tyler!"

Sarah turned to where Russ had shouted as the tall, gangly man strolled over. He was probably about Russ's age, nearly handsome in that thin, washed-out, Tom Petty-ish way.

"Still want that match?" she asked.

"Careful, Tyler," a bystander cut in.

"You got it." He and Sarah pooled their quarters, and he racked, leaving the winner to break. She enjoyed the way his eyebrows jumped as she sent the balls flying across the table.

"Ringer," he said with a laugh.

They played an even game, and Sarah lost with dignity by a single ball. She hadn't been paying very close attention to the game toward the end, her attention glued to Russ in her periphery. He'd had his arms locked over his chest the whole time, a strange look on his face. As she returned her stick and left the table to Tyler and the next challenger, Russ stepped close and took hold of her elbow. "Let's go."

"Sure. Can I just finish my beer—"

"Now."

She felt her brows rise as he led her out the door and into the cold night air, marched her straight to the truck.

"You can let go of my arm, Russ." She said it with a laugh, hoping to lighten the tension now hovering between them.

He released her and they climbed into the cab. He was pissed, but over what, Sarah wasn't sure. The thought annoyed her deeply. She'd had a lovely time, the closest thing to a taste of her old life she'd enjoyed in a month. Maybe Russ didn't think she deserved that. Maybe her overdone triumph at pool or the fun she'd had playing bartender weren't things he thought she had coming to her.

Whatever. He'd invited her. She stared out the window as he drove them into the country, good mood waning, beer buzz turning her from giddy to grouchy.

She was on the verge of nodding off when they pulled into the driveway, predictable barking replacing the drone of the engine. She slammed her door and followed Russ up the steps, patting one of the dogs' heads before kicking her shoes off.

"Thanks," she said as Russ flipped the den lights on. "That was fun."

"Good."

She shut the door and rubbed her arms, wishing a fire were magically there to greet them. "Did *you* have fun?" she asked, eyeing his stern expression.

Russ shrugged and wandered to the sink to pour himself a glass of water. "Yeah. Same old scene, but sure."

"You were awful eager to leave."

She watched him take an almighty breath, gaze trained on the floor.

"What?"

Russ shook his head. "Doesn't matter. I don't want to talk about it."

"Fine." She headed to the couch to get her bed assembled, hoping he'd sleep off whatever was eating him. She'd respect his wishes and take him at face value, not question him to death about what was wrong. Though she sure as hell wanted to know if she'd done anything to trigger this change in the atmosphere between them. Maybe not, though. Maybe he'd just run into somebody he had an old beef with. Who knew what went on in men's heads.

"Got everything you need over there?" he asked, still standing by the kitchen counter.

"Yup."

"Good."

She went to the bathroom to wash her face and brush her teeth. She'd have to do laundry again tomorrow and pray the faint fragrance of other people's smoke came out of her new outfit. As she flipped the bathroom light off, she came face to face with Russ, nearly bumping into him as he headed to his room.

"Sorry," she said. "Bathroom's free."

He nodded, eyes locked on her nose or chin.

"Thanks again." Her words dropped to a whisper as she took in his face from this close up. Those features she thought she knew looked strained. She cleared her throat, reached up and gave his stubbly jaw a playful squeeze. "That's a good look for you."

Russ wrapped his hand around her wrist and held it between their chins. Their eyes darted uncertainly for a handful of seconds, then he leaned in and kissed her.

She felt the brush of his unshaven face, tasted beer and reveled in the slick heat as his tongue slid between her lips. Her gasp died in her throat, and she invited him deeper, as deep as he wanted. He let her hand go and his palm went to her neck, possessiveness heating the gesture.

Whatever he was feeling, she felt it twofold. Longing and animal need, and fear. She wanted this kiss, but knew it wouldn't last. A momentary lapse in Russ's judgment. A surrender. They wouldn't wake to still find this together. She had no doubt of that, though she wouldn't let the chance pass her by, either. She and Russ were temporary, but she wouldn't leave this place having missed any chances to explore with him, physically. To make her interest plain, she took his face in both hands and kissed him back as rough and desperate as he was offering her.

Russ changed. He led her by the shoulders, walking her backward into the den. Their mouths didn't separate until she felt the couch against her calf. He sat first, pulling her gracelessly down to straddle his lap. Forceful hands tugged her hips against his waist and she felt him behind his jeans, hard.

"Russ."

He stroked her shoulders, mouth on her throat.

"Is this what you want?" she muttered.

The sweep of his tongue and the faint drag of his teeth answered her—another wondrous glimpse of the other Russ. Cool air caressed her lower back as he eased her blouse up. She went to work undoing its buttons, then let it drop from her shoulders.

He pulled her close again. "I didn't like seeing you gettin' flirted with by other men." His breath steamed hot against her neck.

"I didn't flirt back."

"I don't care." His hands fumbled with the bra clasp between her shoulder blades, far more rough than competent, far more erotic than any wine-and-candles seduction Sarah's stupid magazines might endorse.

"My body thinks you're mine," he growled, getting the hooks free, hands sliding forward to cup her breasts.

She sucked in a breath, transfixed for a moment, staring at his face and the wildness in his narrowed eyes. Letting him slip the straps down her arms and toss her bra aside, she welcomed the gentle brush of his rough palms. He moaned as she raked his scalp with her nails, a sound she'd missed since he'd taken all this away from them.

"I never stopped wanting you," she whispered, tracing the curves of his ears with her thumbs.

"Me neither."

"You going to regret this tomorrow?"

Russ ran his tongue up her jugular before he spoke. "I don't care."

Good answer. Their entire relationship, if it could be called that, was rooted in spontaneous lapses in judgment. If tonight was to be the culmination of all that, this surrender ought to be one big *what the hell—fuck it* moment too.

Sarah edged her knees back enough to touch him. His chest was firm behind his shirt, ribs rising and falling with labored breaths, stomach tensing under her palms as she memorized him. His thighs flexed, straining. Somehow she'd been given the power to turn this calm, self-possessed grown man into a greedy, panting teenage boy, and she wasn't about to waste it. She slid her hand down over his belt buckle and cupped his stiff cock though his jeans. His back arched as his hips bucked.

"I got something else at the drugstore the other day," she said.

Russ moaned as she squeezed him tighter.

"Probably pretty presumptuous of me—"

"Don't care," he said again.

"Love when you say that. Hang on."

He let her stand, and she went to get the shopping bag from the corner of the room. She opened the condom box and set a strip of them atop the puzzle on the coffee table.

As she made to settle back in his lap, Russ stopped her. "Not here."

"Where?"

He stood, grabbing the condoms. "I want you in my bed."

She licked her lips and followed him, realizing how badly she wanted that too. The most intimate, tangled wilds of Russ's territory. He led her into the dark room to his bed, which she'd made herself that morning, not daring to hope she'd have a hand in desanctifying it so soon. She heard the crinkling of plastic by the bedside table.

"Can we have the lights?" she asked.

A pause, then the lamp beside them clicked on. He held her gaze for a moment then sat beside her.

"Thanks," she mumbled, distracted. He was staring at her, and she had to look a bit silly, half-undressed. She got up to ditch her jeans and underwear, feeling vulnerable in the best way as she sat next to him, her body bare and his still fully clothed.

Some cautiousness returned to Russ when he touched her, his hands gentler now as he held her small breasts, kisses slower and more romantic. She freed her mouth to say, "Let me see you."

Russ's expression cut right into her heart—everything she loved about this man. Loved, indeed. A crazy word to use considering she'd known him less than a week, but the only one that sprang to mind just now. His face was placid, eyes steady, as he unbuttoned his shirt and let it drop, stripped off his tee. Sarah bit her lip, enjoying every square inch of his body as he undressed. She held her breath for the eternity it took for him to unbuckle his belt and open his jeans, push them to the floor along with his shorts. He toed off his socks and kicked them away, but Sarah stopped him before he could sit beside her.

She held him by the hips, enjoying the sheer sight of him. "Just stay there a second." As she explored his body with her eyes and hands, she felt his fingers tangle in her hair. Something about the hunger in that gesture shifted them yet again, banishing the slow, savoring impulses in a heartbeat and ushering the greedy, grasping ones back in. She fisted his cock and held him tight, forgot to breathe as he wrapped his hand around hers. She let him lead, biting back a moan. His hand guided hers, making her feel it as he grew hotter, harder, bigger. This man had come to mean far more to her than just this...but damn, it felt good.

"Russ."

He thrust softly to force her strokes, and the flex of muscle and bone in his hip just about dissolved her brain. She felt his strength and weight, smelled and heard him beside this very bed where they'd come so close to getting what they both wanted. Only not. Nicole had been in the way then, and Sarah was happy now they'd been denied this. If Russ said somebody's name tonight, it'd damn well better be hers. She kneaded his thigh with her free hand, letting her nails dig in and tell him how far beyond ready she'd grown.

He cleared his throat. "I love the way you look at me." He stared her dead in the eyes. "Like you're hungry."

She squeezed him tighter and let him watch as she inventoried the length of his body. "I just want to remember all this."

"For when it's over?"

"For whenever. An hour from now, or tomorrow afternoon. For ten years from now, whether we're strangers then or not."

"Or not?"

"Who knows," she muttered, in no mood for melancholy. "But right now, I just want to enjoy you."

Russ finally let her hand go. "Lie down."

She stretched out across his comforter, body tensing with anticipation as he joined her. He got his knees between hers, and she brought her legs up, locking them to his waist.

"I want to know if this is only about sex for you," Russ said.

"It's not."

"What is it?"

The question scared her, because she knew the answer and how pathetic it would sound. "I just want to know what it's like to be with someone like you. For as long as you let me."

His gaze darted away then held hers, steady. "That's what I want too. You make me feel things... I don't even know how to explain it."

"You don't have to."

Russ's eyes flashed to the side table then back. "I want to please you."

"Lucky me."

He smiled, looking a bit flustered. "What do you need? I mean, I haven't been this riled up in forever. I don't know how... I might not be much good tonight."

She bit back a grin, charmed. "Well, you haven't had any trouble in that department before. What would you *like* to do?"

Thoughts passed over his face and furrowed his brow, then he met her eyes. "Here." Moving to the side, he coaxed her to lie with her back to his chest. He brought his body lower, his thigh spreading her legs, stiff cock sliding against her wet lips. A replay of that wonderful first night in this bed. With his arm wrapped around her waist he found her clit, warm fingertips rubbing soft and slow.

"Russ."

"This okay?"

"That's amazing. So's that," she added, reaching down to run her hand along the ridge of his erection.

"Can't believe how hard you get me."

As his hips pumped in short thrusts that rubbed his stiff flesh against her soft folds, she felt the climax already brewing. His muscles were tensed and hard against her back, breathing shallow. She imagined seeing these same muscles as he braced himself above her, imagined his face as he lost control. Behind her she could sense his mounting excitement, hips speeding along with his stroking fingers.

For a minute or two or ten, she took everything he gave her. As excitement filled her body, fantasies filled her head, perfectly dirty movies of Russ's body working to please her, a live soundtrack right in her ear.

"God, Russ."

"Come on," he whispered. "Please."

Sarah didn't think she'd ever heard a plea that loaded with aggression. She shifted her hips in time with his caresses and felt her body going hot and impatient as the pleasure neared its peak. She imagined how it would look to watch the two of them making love, to see Russ from the side or back or from above as he took her. She palmed his cock and his groan was the final straw. The sensations came to a violent head against his fingertips, an orgasm as harsh and deep and tortured as Russ's voice at her shoulder. She covered his hand as her clit became oversensitive, holding him still as she caught her breath.

With a touch of resistance, Russ let her go. She rolled onto her back, muscles wobbly, and smiled at him. "Your turn."

He nodded and reached for the waiting condom from the table.

"Oh, let me do that." She made grabby-hands at him, eager for any extra excuse to build the anticipation. Russ relinquished it and got to his knees beside her. Leaning close, she pinched the tip and rolled it down his length with the assistance of his impatient hand. Any damper her climax had put on her desire flew out the window as Russ got his knees between hers, angling his cock to her entrance. She held her breath and grasped his shoulders as he pushed the first inch inside.

"Russ."

"Tell me if I need to slow down." He braced his palms beside her ribs and lowered, hips pushing him deeper. A glorious noise rumbled from his throat, the death rattle of seven years' sexual frustration, she bet.

"You feel good," she said, in awe of his face in the lamplight, his firm muscle under her hands. As he slid deeper she felt a pang, but not an entirely unpleasant one.

"You okay?" he asked, eyes on her pursed lips.

"I'm fine. Keep going."

He took the instructions to heart, pushing in the final couple of inches fast and firm. He moaned, eyes shut as he savored. When they opened again his expression turned soft. "Jesus, you're beautiful."

The compliment caught her off guard. "Thanks."

"I'm gonna say something real stupid now," Russ announced, going perfectly still.

"Oh. Alright."

"I'm pretty sure I'm in love with you."

Her mouth fell open. It was as though something hot burst inside her, warmth oozing from her middle out to fill her arms and legs, fingers and toes. It was far too good to be true. Far too much to ever hope that this man felt as strongly about her as she did him.

"And I'm not just saying that because I'm hornier than I've been since tenth grade."

"Okay."

"I'm in love with you. With Sarah," he added firmly. "With the woman who drugged my dogs and robbed me and kicked my ass at pool."

She laughed. "She sounds charming."

Russ grinned, looking a bit relieved that his announcement hadn't scared her.

"She's half in love with you too," Sarah added, the closest she'd ever come to saying those three little loaded words to a man. She stroked his neck and admired his handsome face. She touched his neck, leaned up to kiss him, light and shallow. "Give it another week and she's a goner."

His grin deepened, crinkling the corners of his eyes and giving him a dimple. "Good. I just wanted to say that, in case it slipped out when I lose my mind a couple minutes from now."

"You have my permission. You won't frighten me off."

He nodded then began to thrust, slow and steady. Sarah shut her eyes and simply felt him, all the power and need and surrender in his body and voice. She ran her hands over his back and arms, fisted his hair as he sped up. "Good."

203

"You feel so amazing," he whispered. "I love the way you touch me."

Like you're hungry, her memory echoed. She wanted to give him everything he craved. She slid both hands to his hips, tugging to punctuate each of his thrusts and urge him to be as rough as he liked. Russ accepted the invitation. His moans turned darker and his body grew aggressive. His hips shifted, spreading her wider and taking her deeper. He swore under his breath, and Sarah welcomed it all, drawing her nails across his back.

"Come on, Russ."

"Not yet." He slowed. Grabbing her waist, he rolled them over so he was beneath her.

Sarah grinned at him, pleased by the challenge. She leaned back and set her hands on his belly. "I can't believe you're mine," she said, the words tumbling out of her subconscious.

Russ's eyes looked glazed, and she could feel him inside her, ticking like a bomb. She gave him what he needed, drawing his cock out with a raising of her hips, then taking him back inside. She watched with satisfaction as Russ's hands grasped the pillow beneath his head.

As she took him, Sarah felt her desire growing again, stronger than before. "How close are you?"

"Dunno," Russ said, then gasped as she welcomed him deep again.

"Could you hold on maybe two minutes?"

He nodded wildly, looking incapable of speech.

She lowered down, bracing her hands beside Russ's shoulders. The angles came naturally with him, and Sarah found what she needed, the brush of his pubic bone against her clit as she rode him. His hands cupped her breasts, and he raised his knees, scooting her forward and intensifying the friction between their bodies. She gave in to the feeling, dropping to her elbows and burying her face against his neck.

"You feel so good," she whispered. She savored him, getting lost in everything masculine about him—deep voice, hard cock, strong muscles. She shoved her hands beneath his shoulders and dug her fingers into him, never wanting to let go. She hadn't removed the necklace and its beads bit into the skin of her throat, beautiful. Russ moved his palms to her waist, following the greedy motions of her hips. As he began to thrust back, she lost it. Just that little taste of how needy and turned on he was threw her headlong toward a second climax.

"Russ."

His hands and hips kept her riding him as the pleasure peaked. His aggression burned just as hot as the friction and penetration, and Sarah heard herself moaning as she came, the orgasm so intense it bordered on painful.

"Oh God." She found herself back in reality, sweaty chest plastered to Russ's, the quiet room filled with the heat and the smell of them. She pushed up to stare at his flushed face, and he tucked her hair behind her ears and raised his head and shoulders to kiss her chin.

"Wow. It's so your turn."

He urged her to roll over again, gentler this time. As she felt his weight on top of her, Sarah had a moment of intense clarity, a realization more potent and irrefutable than she'd ever felt before.

She stared straight into his eyes. "I love you."

He said nothing, but his eyes stayed on hers, steady.

An urge to cry struck her, tingling in her sinuses. She'd always thought is was a load of baloney when movies showed people professing their devotion in bed, making love as opposed to good old-fashioned screwing. Now here that was, happening to her—to Sarah Novak from the crappiest, most dead-end corner of Buffalo. Before the tears could come she turned herself over to Russ, hugging her legs tight around his hips and hugging his cock deep inside her core.

He took the hint, eyes leaving her face to study her breasts and the view between their bodies. Tiny indentions traced an upside-down arch below his collarbone—the impressions of her necklace's beads. He moved gently and slowly inside her.

Sarah bit her lip and smiled up at him. "Don't go all tender on me now, just because we're suddenly making love."

He laughed softly. "Forgot what you said before, about never fucking you like a lady."

"Damn straight."

She thought she'd die right then as Russ's arms tensed beside her, muscles standing out dramatically in the lamplight. He gave her exactly what she wanted, that hot, fast, mean slap of his body against hers and the forceful thrust of his cock as he finally put his pleasure first.

She stroked his chest as she studied his face. "Good."

"I'm so close." His hips sped into the home stretch, rough and perfect.

Sarah watched his abdomen as he hammered her, and raked his skin with her nails just to draw a final gasp from him.

"Yes." His entire body froze, cock buried as deep as it went, eyes shut tight. Three tremors tightened and released him, and Russ sighed, eyes opening to stare down at her. For once, no regret lurked in his expression, just sex-drunk bliss.

Sarah stroked his face and brushed his hair from his eyes. "Good." She traced his lips and they widened into a smile. He withdrew and got rid of the condom. When he returned he tugged the covers from beneath them and rolled them onto their sides. Cocooning their bodies together, he kissed her lightly as his breathing slowed. She placed a hand over his heart to feel its racing beats, keeping it there until the rhythm slowed to a faint murmur. Russ nodded off ages before she did, leaving her to bask in this extraordinary moment until she, too, finally joined him in the sweet oblivion.

Chapter Thirteen

Russ woke earlier than usual to find his arms locked tight around Sarah beneath the covers. For a minute his heart pounded, then eased. He'd given in. It was done, the decision turned over to his heart, and thank goodness. He didn't care what she was to him anymore, or how long she'd be in his life. All he cared about was the way she looked at him, how alive he felt when they shared a ride or a meal or a bed.

Peeling his arm from her waist as gently as he could, he craned his body, hoping to turn off the impending alarm. She stirred and made a sleepy noise, and he froze, not wanting to rouse her.

"You awake?" he whispered.

"Mmm-hmm."

He pressed his lips to her neck, breathed her in. After a few seconds' silence he mumbled, "Thank you."

She turned over to smile at him, eyes bleary. "What for?"

"For last night...after I was so wishy-washy about it that other night, then acted like a jackass at the bar."

She laughed and reached back to pat his head awkwardly. "You're allowed to be wishy-washy about sleeping with fugitives. That sounds wise. And you're very much allowed to act like a jackass if it means you're going to drag me home all jealous and give me what I want."

"Anytime."

"Oh good." She turned away, pressing her back into Russ's chest, pure heaven.

He cleared his throat and emptied his brain of a few thoughts that'd been brewing since the ride home from the bar. "Are you happy here?"

She nodded against the pillow. "I am."

"And you think you'll stick around for a while?"

She rolled over again to face him. "Yeah. I don't want to go, Russ. I want to stay for a while, like you offered, help you out and earn my keep."

"How long's a while?"

She shrugged, lips pursed shyly. "As long as my back holds up?"

"Winters are real long and cold."

"Can't be worse than Buffalo."

He smirked at that.

"I don't know," she said, expression turning sad. "Right now, naked in bed with you or outside under that gigantic sky...this is better than anything I could go back and find in New York. But it's impractical. We both know that."

His heart sank. "Yeah."

"We can play house for a month or a year, but eventually something will happen. We'll need to travel, or I'll have to go to the hospital or drive you someplace, and the fact that I don't want to share my ID with anyone is going to get problematic. And trust me, I'm leaving before I have a chance to get you into trouble for it."

Russ entertained a couple of desperate, ridiculous schemes—paying for false paperwork, running off to Mexico with her. He sighed. Even in the most candy-coated of all outcomes, he couldn't ever marry her, not without somebody someplace running her social security number through a series of legal checks. He envied his forefathers intensely at that moment, living in eras when every last movement a person made wasn't linked to some computer system. She was right. This couldn't ever be practical, not unless she went back and faced the music, and served who-knew-how-many years for what she'd gotten tangled up in. That thought hurt nearly as badly as the idea of never seeing her again once she left—this vibrant woman left to wither in a prison cell. Still, one thing scared him worse.

"I hate thinking of what it'll be like for you, after you leave. Out there, wherever 'there' is."

Her eyes snapped back and forth between each of his. "It scares me, too."

"What if... Maybe nothing bad *would* happen. If you stayed."

In the faint dawn light he saw her brows rise, intrigued or skeptical.

"Maybe you could stay here indefinitely. Help me out around the property, maybe get Harry to pay you under the table to bartend a couple nights a week, so you don't feel like you owe so much?"

She smiled weakly. "Then one day I break my arm and you can't fix it with your little vet kit, and the hospital staff wants to know who they're checking in. Then you go to jail right alongside me for being an accomplice or harboring a fugitive or whatever."

His chest deflated, and he nodded, knowing she was right.

"I don't know what's going to happen, Russ. It's a relief just to be able to stay still for a while, and I'd like to enjoy that while it lasts. And I'd like to stay with you, at least for the winter. I'll just be real careful about injuring myself too grievously."

"Okay."

"And if something does happen... I want you to tell the police you had no idea who I really am. Tell them you know only what we made up last night, that stuff about Florida. I want you to promise me you won't throw yourself under the bus with me if something goes wrong. I'll bet you've never lied before in your life, but if that ever happens, lie. Promise me."

He looked past her face to the pink light slipping through the blinds.

"Russ."

"I don't know if I can promise that. Not if telling the authorities *you* lied to *me* this whole time could make things worse for you."

She took a deep breath and blew it out. "Well, if that day ever does come, I hope you'll think of your family first. And everyone around here who relies on you."

Russ buried his face between her neck and the pillow, exhausted by this conversation. Terrified of the day he might watch her walk away from him and into who-knew-what, out there in the larger world. Terrified of being alone again after feeling what he did with her. He wished he had it in him to turn her in. At least he'd know she'd be safe. Or safe-ish, depending on what women's prison was like... But he understood her well enough to believe that losing her freedom would damage her worse than losing her sense of safety.

"You're right," he said, words muffled. "Let's enjoy the winter. Let's just enjoy this for however long it lasts."

She ran her fingers through his messy hair. "Good. And more importantly than that, let's enjoy today. For all we know, it could be our last one together."

"In that case, I'm making us pancakes."

She smiled. "I won't stop you."

"Then as soon as the horses are tended to, we're riding out to the river and I'm going to give you what we talked about before. You and me, outside, under all that sky."

She laughed. "It's got to be in the midfifties out there."

"We'll build a bonfire."

Her grin turned shy. "Okay. I'd like that. Then later this morning I want to finish those curtains and maybe make you a matching tablecloth if there's enough of that fabric left over."

Russ had to grin himself at such a domestic proposition. "That sounds lovely. Bring this place into the twenty-first century." He kissed her forehead, then her cheek. When he reached her mouth his priorities shifted, the thought of pancakes and curtains dissolving. Just as things were heating up, the alarm began to shriek. Russ swore, leaned over and slapped it off.

"Where were we?" Sarah asked.

He was all set to remind her when another ruckus spoiled the moment. The dogs began to bark, and he caught the unmistakable grind of tires against gravel. He cursed again and left the bed to yank his shorts up his legs.

The doorbell sounded as he reached the living room. Russ glanced out the window and spotted Ben's cruiser parked alongside his truck. His heart dropped into his feet.

He ran back to the bedroom threshold, barely breathing. "The police are here." The bell chimed again.

Sarah's eyes went round, amber circles with white all around them. "Oh my God."

"Go to the barn and hide."

"What'll you do?"

"I don't know, but go. Now. I'll find you when it's safe to come out. If I shout at the dogs, that means he's with me and you should stay put, okay?"

She nodded.

He grabbed his robe from the hook and thrust it at her. "Hurry. Before he goes around back looking for me." He turned to the den and bellowed, "Hang on!"

She shoved her arms into the sleeves and ran for the back door, closing it quietly.

Russ looked down at himself and decided this ensemble actually worked rather well for the circumstances. He jogged to the front door, took a breath and opened it.

Ben grinned at him through the screen, beady brown eyes taking in his getup, or lack thereof. "Catch you at a bad time, Russ?"

"Just woke up. Sorry. Couldn't find my robe. What can I do for you so early, Ben?"

"I've come to talk to your guest, actually. Sarah."

"Oh really?" Russ hoped against bizarre hope. "This a social call?"

"'Fraid not. More of a missing-person-type issue. I got some questions for her."

"Oh."

"So, if you don't mind me coming in..." Ben opened the screen door.

"She's gone," Russ blurted.

"Gone? 'Til when?"

"I dunno, actually. She disappeared late last night, left a thank-you note and half the tips she made off Harry." Wait. Shit. *Please don't ask to see the note.* "Other day she was asking me what the best route was to take to Canada, but I didn't think anything of it...thought we were just talking."

Ben swore and shook his head, looking pissed. Looking like he believed Russ. "This is real unfortunate."

"Apparently."

"That girl's in some nasty kind of trouble, as best I can gather," Ben said. "Thought something was fishy about her first time I saw you two in the parking lot. She seemed real evasive at the bar too. I got to talking with Tyler about her, and he pointed out she had a mighty funny accent for a Florida girl. So I ran some checks. I don't know about no Sarah Roberts, but there's a Sarah Novak who used to tend bar in upstate New York and a lot of people are looking for her. They found her phone and bank card in a restaurant trash can in Des Moines."

"Oh?"

"Your houseguest ain't who she says she is, Russ."

"Wow. I really don't know what to—"

An electronic ping interrupted them, and Ben pulled his phone from his belt holster. "Yeah? This ain't the best time, actually... Shit. Anybody hurt bad? Goddamn, your timing couldn't be worse. Uh-huh. Yeah, I know it ain't. Okay, fine." He clipped the phone in its place. "Fuck it all. I gotta go, but I need to talk to you some more. It's real important we find that girl."

"Right, well—"

"I'll be by again soon as I can." Ben let the door hiss closed and turned to Russ as he clomped down the front steps. "I dunno what she told you, Russ, but she ain't who she says she is. You call me. And if she contacts you or comes back, for the love of God, keep her here, however you have to."

Russ watched until the cruiser disappeared then bolted for the back door. He stubbed his toe on the steps and burst into the barn, treading in God knew what. "Sarah?"

She emerged from behind a stack of bales, hugging the robe tight around her. "He's gone?"

"Yeah. He got called off for some accident. He knows who you are. We have to move fast."

She hurried forward. "What do we do?"

"You pack everything you have while I toss some hay and water at the horses. Then I drive you to Billings and we get you on a bus."

"What if they need ID?"

"I'll buy the ticket...or you can use your fake license. I dunno. We just pray it works out. And if it doesn't, I'll drive you as far as I can, okay?"

She shook her head. "I don't want you involved like that. They could figure out where you went, somehow."

"I'll pretend I had other business in the city. Don't worry about that. Just get dressed and get your stuff together, grab some food for the road and meet me at the truck in five minutes."

She nodded and went inside. Russ followed, throwing on some clothes. He did the bare minimum he could get away with for the horses and dogs, and found Sarah waiting for him at the truck.

"You better be ready to scrunch down as low as you can once we're on the road, in case we pass somebody."

She nodded and climbed in.

Russ's heart pounded as he opened his door. He grabbed a pad and pen from the glovebox and scribbled a note.

Ben—had to run off on a job. Call me if you need anything.

He intentionally left out his cell phone number, thinking maybe that'd buy him a few extra minutes if need be. He dashed to the door and slid the paper in the frame of the screen.

Sarah looked pale and thin in the passenger seat so Russ concentrated on driving, afraid to glance at her and see that fear in her eyes. Too heartbreaking. Too damn painful, looking at what he was about to lose. Fucking hell, he was supposed to be making her pancakes right now. He wasn't supposed to be driving her right out of his life, no time for goodbyes.

He took a back road, a truck route that'd take them off-course at first, but avoid the town and most of the traffic. A dozen fresh, hopeful, deluded ideas flashed through Russ's mind.

Maybe he could run away with her... No. Impossible. Maybe he could drive her to his folks' place. No, even worse. This couldn't be happening...not this soon. Not this way. And it was a hundred percent his fault too, for inviting her to that party right under the goddamn deputy's nose. Idiot. Head foggy with guilt and fear and selfish anger over losing her, he aimed them toward the first of a dozen rural routes that would take them back to Billings, take this woman out of his life forever.

Jesus, that sky. Sarah drank it in, all that blue, and tried to fill her brain and overdose on it and never wake back up to face reality.

The reality was, she was in love with Russ. Twenty-seven and in love for the first time, yet it felt like a curse. Such a wonderful gift under other circumstances, but here and now it was unbearably heavy, a burden. A gift she'd done nothing to deserve, and how poetic that it should be taken away like this. How cruel that if Russ really did feel that way for her, now he was feeling the same pain. Once again, something she was stealing from him. She might one day go to jail for manslaughter, but if there was a hell she'd surely be checking in as a thief.

Coward. Selfish as well. So the opposite of what Russ deserved. She stole a glance at him and it stung. How did that quote go? *Better to have loved and lost...* Bullshit. At this moment, she wished she'd never met him. She wished she'd left her phone at home that last night in Buffalo, and that she was still there now. Still trapped in her big concrete pen and in her unremarkable life, Russ still hundreds of miles away, safe.

Better her free and him lonely than both of them forced to say goodbye this way.

Twice he'd be losing a woman he loved. She considered what he'd said about losing his wife, and how unfair it felt to him, how angry it made him. Was this less fair, she wondered? His wife had been taken away by chance. Sarah was being taken away, and she couldn't blame it on her former friend or that horrible man. Perhaps an accident had taken away her freedom, but what she had with Russ, she was the one taking that away, letting her fear dictate her decision and choosing to wreck any chance at a future she might have with this extraordinary man. Fear of imprisonment and fear that he wouldn't want her when she might one day be released... Her mother had been a frightened person, and she'd always chosen to hide, in drugs and inside her own head. Sarah had grown into such a similar woman, frightened and desperate, and not only was she hiding, she was running as well. Surviving was no way to live. Surviving was merely existing, and Sarah didn't want that, anymore. She wanted to thrive, the way she'd felt this past glorious week with Russ.

"Russ."

He swallowed but didn't reply.

"Russ."

He met her eyes with his fearful ones. "You forget something?"

She shook her head and Russ looked back to the road.

"I want you to take me to the station." Her voice sounded far away to her own ears, disembodied.

"I am."

"No, Russ, the sheriff's station."

She watched his face as the needle in his brain scratched all the way across its record, his thoughts surely feeling as scrambled as hers had before she'd committed to this decision.

He slowed the truck and pulled onto the overgrown shoulder. "What?"

She looked him dead in the eyes. "I want to turn myself in."

"You said that scared you worse than anything. That it wasn't an option."

"It does scare me. It terrifies me. But how long can I run for, before this happens again? I mean..." She trailed off then took a mighty breath, composing herself. "I can survive prison, if I know I might get to see you again on the other side."

"You've got no idea what your sentence is, though."

She shook her head. "I have no idea about anything anymore, except that I fell in love with a good man out here, and if I do the right thing now I'll have some chance of seeing him again someday. If he stills wants me."

Russ's features shifted, face overcome by pain at what she'd said. He leaned forward to touch her jaw, kissing her hard and quick. "He will."

"Then I want to go to the station, please."

Russ breathed deeply for a few minutes, and she let him battle with his thoughts, just as she'd done.

"I'm sure, Russ."

He sighed, blank gaze fixed on the steering wheel.

"This is what I want. I'm done running."

He closed his eyes through another deep breath then leaned back in his seat. "Okay. We can go to the station, if you're *sure* that's what you want."

"It is, thank you."

Russ opened his eyes and seemed to steady himself. He made a U-turn and aimed them toward town.

Sarah watched the faded greens and tans of the autumn countryside stream past, mourning these sights. Mourning the proximity of Russ's body. She let her eyes drink in the hugeness of the sky, rolled down her window to swallow gulps of the cool air to ease the tightness of her throat. She hated this sensation. Her claustrophobia was kicking in already, invisible hands wringing her neck. This was how he'd see her for the last time in who knew how long…hyperventilating and mottled with hives. But if there was some chance she'd be able to see him one day as a truly free woman, she'd swallow her pride and fight through her worst fears to claim it.

Far too quickly, the town's church spire appeared beyond the trees. She glanced at Russ, his eyes glued to the road. She reached out and touched him, rubbing his side through his shirt. She caught his nostrils flare and wondered if he might be as close to tears as she was.

"Don't be sad," she said.

"I'm gonna feel like such a shit, leaving you in there."

"You're a good man, Russ. You've done so much more for me than I ever deserved… Now I'm going to do right by you. If we're supposed to see each other again, it'll be when things are fixed. Or as fixed as I can make them."

Russ didn't reply, just turned them onto the main street, truck slowing noticeably as they neared their destination. He parked on the street a block from the sheriff's station but Sarah cut him off before he could tempt her into changing her mind.

"I'm sure, Russ. Let's go."

He took a deep breath and drove them into the small lot, seeming to park as far from the cruiser as possible. Russ's phone buzzed but he ignored it.

"So," he said.

This is goodbye. "Yeah, so."

"I can come in with you."

She shook her head. "I don't want you to see me when they do whatever they do. And I don't want you saying the wrong thing and implicating yourself. I want you to go home, and if they ask you what happened, say I came back and asked you to please drive me to the station. Okay?"

With what looked like a painful effort, Russ nodded. "Here..." He dug in his wallet and came out with a business card. "In case there's bail or however that works. Or if you need anything. For me to find you a lawyer. Anything. Or for when you have a chance to make a phone call, for whatever reason."

She smiled as genuinely as she could and tucked it in her wallet. "Right. Well."

"I'll um... I'll hang on to your things. For whenever you're ready to get them."

She nodded, not wanting to ponder how long that might be. She pictured her new clothes and shoes stacked neatly in that dark room, collecting dust after Russ shut the door on yet another chance at happiness.

He undid his seatbelt and opened his door, meeting her as she hopped down from the truck. His hug was fierce and comforting, as warm and strong as she needed it to be just now.

"I'll miss you," she whispered.

"Me too. I love you."

She laughed against his shoulder, needing to be brave. "You've got awful taste in women...but I love you too. You take care of yourself." She felt him nod. As she let him go, the cold enveloped her and the unseen hands closed tight around her throat once more. She touched his still-stubbly face, took in those green-gray eyes one last time.

He rubbed her arms, mustering a weak smile. "I'll be a wreck until I know what's happening. Call me as soon as you can."

"I will. Maybe I'll see you in court. Who knows."

He nodded, and Sarah found the ability to move, walking backward toward the station, watching him grow farther and farther away. As she reached the steps she mouthed, "I love you," and pulled the door open. Russ put his fingers to his lips and held them up, then tucked his hands in his pockets as she disappeared inside the tiny building.

The office was empty, and she took a deep breath, glancing around. A few wanted posters were hung on the wall, none of them hers, though the ones featuring mug shots filled her gut with ice water. Then, with a feeling of the oddest relief, she stepped to the desk and tapped the silver bell.

She heard a filing cabinet roll shut, and a rotund man with a gray mustache whom she hadn't met at the party appeared from a side room. He did a double take. "Sarah?"

She nodded. "Yeah. I'm Sarah Novak. Your deputy's looking for me."

"Yes, indeed he is. He just went up to Russ Gray's place to collect you." In a gesture that shocked her, the sheriff leaned over the cluttered desk to offer his hand. Dumbstruck, she shook it.

"I'm Sheriff Walters. Have a seat." He waved at a desk chair a few feet away, and she rolled it closer, trying to look obedient and harmless and deserving of a minimum sentence.

"Sounds like a lot of people have been looking for you for quite a while," he said. "You in some trouble you want to tell me about?"

She nodded, happy he was playing Good Cop. She'd gratefully play Good Criminal right back. "Yeah. I'd like to turn myself in. Please. And I'd like a lawyer, before I say too much else."

His eyebrows rose. "A lawyer?"

"Yes. I'm pretty sure that's my right."

He scratched his chin. "Wait. And you said you're turning yourself in?"

She nodded. "Will someone be assigned to me? Because I don't have any money."

"Sorry, Miss Novak, but I don't really understand what you're asking me."

Her confidence faltered. "I want to have a lawyer here, before I get charged or however it works."

"Only criminals need lawyers, sweetheart. You been watching too many police dramas?" he asked, smiling.

She bit her tongue before she could blurt, *But I am a criminal.* Instead she said, "Why am I here exactly? Your deputy was looking for me. Russ told me so, after I told him I needed a ride here. After I ran off," she added lamely, trying to juggle her stories, unsure what was going on.

The sheriff leaned back and his chair creaked mournfully. "You got to know why you're here. You been gone for what, a month now? Ben found you in the Missing Persons database. You've got a whole bunch of worried people back in New York who got no idea where you ran off to."

"Oh."

"So I'll have the honor of letting folks know you've been found. Lucky me. Now if you're in some kind of trouble," he said, leaning on his desk and giving her a sage, fatherly look, "you can feel free to tell me about it. We're here to help you, you know. Ben said you lied about where you were from, and I can't imagine that's a good sign. Now, if you need to be put in touch with a domestic-abuse case worker...or substance abuse?"

She felt her eyes grow wide. "No, definitely not. I just...I think there's been a misunderstanding. I don't suppose you could look something up for me? If I give you somebody's name? There was this guy back home that I was afraid of..."

"Okie dokie, hang on." The sheriff jiggled his mouse to wake his computer, typed and clicked for a minute. "All righty, what's this fella's name?"

"His last name was Drew. I don't know his first name... Everyone called him T, though. He's from Buffalo."

He punched some keys. "Drew...Buffalo... Tomas Drew? Hospitalized August twenty-eight for a concussion, accidental, then convicted on an outstanding warrant for possession and distribution of illicit substances and assault. That sound like the guy?"

She blinked. "Oh. Yes, it does."

"Well, with a previous conviction he's looking at four and a half to nine years, mandatory minimum for New York. Don't think you need to worry about him for a while. Unless he's got some friends...?"

"No, no... It says the concussion was accidental?"

"Yup. That's pretty common in drug-related disturbances. So-called big shots refuse to rat each other out."

Or admit a girl took them down, Sarah wagered. "Well... I um, I was worried about him, if I went back home. I sort of freaked out, I'm afraid. That's why I ran away."

"Put yourself under homemade witness protection?" the sheriff teased.

She smiled weakly, confusion and hope and disbelief expanding in her ribs, too fast and too full. "I guess. But anyhow, am I just free to go, or...?"

"Course. I'll need you to sign a statement, and you'll want to make some phone calls, I imagine. Let everybody know you're okay? And we can chat more about social services, for when you go back."

"Yeah, of course. Listen..."

"Mm-hmm?"

Determined not to lie ever again, Sarah struggled for the words. "Russ didn't know about all this...that guy's conviction and all that stuff... When I first ended up at his place, he only took me in to be kind, and let me help out to make some money..." Unable to figure out a truthful way to cobble in the last of the details, she trailed off, hoping the sheriff might fill in the rest.

"I'm sure he didn't. Russ is the last guy I've ever suspect of knowingly harboring a missing person. Don't you worry, he's not in trouble."

"Oh, good."

"So let me get you set up with a phone in the break room, and you can spread the good news to all those worried friends of yours, okay? And I'll get the paperwork sorted out so we can get you off that missing-persons list."

"Okay. Is there someone who could drive me to Russ's afterward?"

"Sure. I'll do it myself, as soon as Ben's back from his call."

"Great. Thank you. Thank you so much."

Russ set the hose aside, checking his phone for the hundredth time since he'd dropped Sarah off. Nothing. Not even Ben had called; the message he'd received in the sheriff's parking lot had been about setting up an overdue dentist appointment. He went back to his chores, lost in the details, more lost in his thoughts. Lost in images of Sarah in handcuffs, in court, in prison with no hope of parole.

Beside him, Tulah jumped to her feet, ears perked. She barked.

"Shush." He checked his phone again. Nothing. He checked the battery and the reception bars, both strong. He sighed then started as Tulah went nuts, setting Kit off in the distance. He heard the source of their excitement, tires on gravel. *Ben.* Russ took a steadying breath and wiped his hands on a horse blanket, hoping he didn't look as gutted as he felt.

He raised his hand as the cruiser trundled to a halt. To his surprise, Sheriff Walters himself emerged. To his vastly greater surprise, Sarah appeared from the passenger side.

"Whoa."

"Howdy, Russ!"

"Heya, Sheriff. What's—" He shut up as Sarah put a finger to her lips behind the sheriff's back.

"Little lady re-enters civilized society and who does she want to see first? Lucky man."

Russ forced a smile to cover his incomprehension.

Sarah walked up to him, gaze volleying between the two men. "Thanks for the lift, and all the help," she said to the sheriff.

He tipped his hat to her. "Call if you need anything. You're the most exciting thing that'll happen all season, I'm sure." He turned and nodded. "Russ."

"Sheriff."

Russ and Sarah stood side by side and watched until the cruiser was replaced with a cloud of dust. He looked to his right, mystified by how it was that she was standing here.

"I'm free," she said softly.

"How?" He whispered it, as though they might somehow be under surveillance.

"The guy I assaulted...he didn't die. And he didn't press charges. He's in prison for drug trafficking and nobody reported me for having anything to do with it."

Russ blinked for a few seconds, trying to turn the words she'd said into coherent thoughts.

"They were looking for me because I was on a missing-persons registry for disappearing."

"What?"

She took his hand in both of hers, thumbs rubbing his knuckles. "Russ, I'm sorry. I've made the last week hell for you, when I should have figured out a way to find all this out for myself. Or turned myself in soon—"

He cut her apologies off with a kiss, folding her into his arms and wishing he never had to let go. After a long time he released her to arm's length, studying her face. "So you're free."

"I'm free... And I'm staying, if you'll let me."

His heart stuttered. He took her hand and led her to the porch steps to take a seat. He kept their thighs and hips touching, afraid she might float away on the cold fall breeze if he didn't keep them physically connected. Clearing his throat, he managed to form words. "You don't want to go back home?"

"There's not much for me, back there...my old job, a few friends, more trouble. Maybe here I could take a couple odd jobs, help you with the animals. Maybe save up and buy a car and take classes someplace. I dunno. I feel like I can do anything, now. Like this is that fresh start I always fantasized about. But for now, maybe for the winter, I'd like to just stay here like I have been, helping you. Thinking about what I want."

His hopes sank. "So you think it's temporary? A few months?"

"A few months of chores, getting the hang of things before I think about going back to school. But staying with you...I'd like to do that for as long as you want me, Russ." She scanned the sky, eyes lit up in the sun. "It's only been a week, but I can't imagine leaving here." Her gaze moved to his face. "Or you."

Warm air seemed to fill his chest, so full Russ thought he might just float away himself.

"I better come up with a good excuse for lying about being from Florida, I guess," she added, smiling.

Ideas pummeled Russ left and right. "We need to get you some more clothes...a winter coat. Oh, and better-fitting boots and a saddle."

She laughed. "Yeah. Let's get me outfitted... I'll pay you back in chores, or tips if the bar wants my help."

"I don't care," Russ said, and pulled her against him once more. He felt the chilly skin of her cheek against his neck and released her. "You're freezing. Let's get you inside."

She nodded. "Let's get me home."

Russ took her hand and led her up the steps and into the warmth. He watched her wander through the den, taking everything in as a free woman. In turn he studied her, this person so suddenly allowed to be here with him. Miraculous.

All at once, everything felt wrong. Well, not everything. Not Sarah, but this room. This house. Russ looked at the dated wood paneling and the old furniture, all the trappings of a life so stale it wasn't even his—purchased and settled into along with the rest of this home. He'd gotten dangerously comfortable in this space, alone in his routines and duties, his waiting. Sarah had just avoided a cell, and here they were standing in Russ's.

"I want you to decorate," he said, putting his hands to his hips.

She turned to smile at him. "Sure."

"Change it. All of it."

She flopped onto his couch, hair bouncing. "Even this squishy old thing?"

"Yeah."

"But I like it. It's so soft and full of memories."

"We'll make other memories, on some other couch. We'll break it in ourselves." He pictured too much, then—relatives visiting, proud introductions, Sarah in a cap and gown for some yet-unknown accomplishment, then perhaps another kind of gown. Children clambering, barbecues outside and laughter within these walls once again. As much beauty and freedom inside this home as there was beyond its windows. Far too much to think about, yet too much felt wonderful. Russ was as overwhelmed with hope now as he had been with dread just minutes earlier.

"Feel like I'm dreaming," he muttered. "Or drunk."

"Me too."

She patted the spot next to her, and Russ rounded the coffee table to take a seat. He leaned forward, elbows on his knees, and stared at the puzzle still spread across the wood. He felt like that puzzle, left to rattle around in the musty dark for years, now slowly being put back together, his picture not entirely clear but already promising to be bright and cheerful. Possibly plagued by a hole or two, but that was only to be expected. He poured over individual pieces then reached out, pressing a segment of solid blue sky into its place.

"This is awfully poetic," Sarah said. "You helping me make sense of all this chaos." She shook the box lid, filled with hundreds of steps en route to completion.

"I was thinking something like that." He moved a few more slices of sky around, really only aware of the warmth of her body next to his, and of all the space he could feel opening up in his chest. So much room, suddenly. She wrapped her arm around his back and joined him in sliding bits of landscape here and there, auditioning grass against grass, water against water.

"We've got the real thing outside," he finally said. He sensed her nodding. "You feel like a ride?"

When he turned he found her smiling, the corners of her eyes crinkling. "Sure."

He made them a Thermos of coffee and assembled two sandwiches, and they got the horses ready. As Russ slowed Mitch to let Sarah draw up beside him, he thought she just about fit, out here. He felt excited for the life she might choose to build for herself...tending bar, making dresses, perhaps something altogether unexpected. It was joyful to stand beside someone at the threshold of a new life, to wonder alongside them what the future held, to feel all that hope blooming large in his own chest. He knew as well as anyone that there were no guarantees, no insurance available that could promise a life free of loss, be that loss violent and senseless or meticulously planned. All one could do was live, to plan and hope for good things, and to take the bad in stride, with eyes wide open.

Her voice pulled him out of his head. "It's not like me to think this way, but I feel like maybe everything that happened back in Buffalo was for a reason. For the best, in its own perverted way."

"Maybe."

"Figures my higher power would have a sadistic streak," she teased.

"Well, if you make it through a Montana winter without losing your mind, I've got high hopes for you."

"Me too."

"But I'll buy you a TV for Christmas, just in case."

She laughed. "Probably wise."

Christmas, he thought. And Thanksgiving. Sarah beside him in the truck, heading for Idaho. Beside him anywhere, though—that was gift enough. He led them forward, into the familiar and the unknown, under a sky too wide to measure. Everything mundane, everything mysterious. Everything so exactly as it should be.

About the Author

Before becoming a writer, Meg worked as a record store bitch, a lousy barista, a decent designer, and an over-enthusiastic penguin handler. She loves writing sexy, character-driven stories about strong-willed men and women who keep each other on their toes...and bring one another to their knees.

Meg now writes full-time and lives north of Boston with her extremely good-natured and permissive husband. When she's not trapped in her own head, she can usually be found in the kitchen, the coffee shop, or jogging around the nearest duck-filled pond.

Meg welcomes reader feedback. E-mail her at meg@megmaguire.com, follow her on Twitter @megguire, or visit her website at www.megmaguire.com.

Secretly wanting her—no problem.
Her not-so-secretly wanting him—big trouble.

Just My Type
© *2010 Erin Nicholas*
The Bradfords, Book 3

There's only one problem with the woman Jason "Mac" Gordon wants: his best friend's little sister is off limits. Way off limits, and too young and innocent for the likes of him. From past experience, he's learned to hide his not-so-nice preferences from the nice girls he seems to attract. That definitely includes the woman he's always thought of as a sister. At least until recently.

Sara Bradford always gets what she wants—which is partly Mac's fault. After all, he helped spoil her. So she has no intention of taking his no for an answer on anything—least of all his refusal to sleep with her. He thinks she's too innocent? Fine. She'll simply get un-innocent and show Mac that she wants him—the good, the bad and the nipple clamps.

When Mac's plan to drive her away works too well, he's forced to follow her to a tropical paradise, determined to make sure she doesn't find her wild side with anyone but him. Once she gets a real taste of what he likes, he's sure everything will go back to normal.

That's until he discovers a slight kink, er, flaw in his logic…

Warning: Contains hot sex at the beach, kinky online shopping—and yes, cotton-candy-flavored body powder does exist.

Available now in ebook and print from Samhain Publishing.

It's all about the story...

Romance

HORROR

www.samhainpublishing.com

CPSIA information can be obtained at www.ICGtesting.com
Printed in the USA
BVOW041825220512

290849BV00001B/2/P